'Paige will be waiting. . .'

Then Niall looked up at Jess and smiled, that heart-warming, heart-stopping smile that was all the things that Jess considered most dangerous in a man.

'Ten minutes, Dr Harvey,' he smiled. 'Ten minutes more of human contact before I go back to being the Ogre of Barega.'

He knew. He knew of his reputation.

Jessie felt herself flush crimson but Niall Mountmarche was smiling in a way that showed he didn't mind in the least—in fact, by the look of it, he rather liked it!

GW00708153

Marion Lennox has had a variety of careers—medical receptionist, computer programmer and teacher. Married, with two young children, she now lives in rural Victoria, Australia. Her wish for an occupation which would allow her to remain at home with her children and her dog led her to begin writing, and she has now published a number of medical romances.

Recent titles by the same author:

PRESCRIPTION—ONE HUSBAND
BUSH DOCTOR'S BRIDE
A CHRISTMAS BLESSING
ENCHANTING SURGEON
DANGEROUS PHYSICIAN
DOCTOR'S HONOUR

PRESCRIPTION—
ONE BRIDE

BY
MARION LENNOX

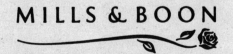

DID YOU PURCHASE THIS BOOK WITHOUT A COVER?
If you did, you should be aware it is **stolen property** as it was
reported *unsold and destroyed* by a retailer. Neither the Author nor
the publisher has received any payment for this book.

*All the characters in this book have no existence outside the imagination
of the author, and have no relation whatsoever to anyone bearing the
same name or names. They are not even distantly inspired by any
individual known or unknown to the author, and all the incidents are
pure invention.*

*All rights reserved including the right of reproduction in whole or in
part in any form. This edition is published by arrangement with
Harlequin Enterprises II B.V. The text of this publication or any part
thereof may not be reproduced or transmitted in any form or by any
means, electronic or mechanical, including photocopying, recording,
storage in an information retrieval system, or otherwise, without the
written permission of the publisher.*

*This book is sold subject to the condition that it shall not, by way of
trade or otherwise, be lent, resold, hired out or otherwise circulated
without the prior consent of the publisher in any form of binding or
cover other than that in which it is published and without a similar
condition including this condition being imposed on the subsequent
purchaser.*

*MILLS & BOON, the Rose Device and
LOVE ON CALL are trademarks of the publisher.
Harlequin Mills & Boon Limited,
Eton House, 18-24 Paradise Road, Richmond, Surrey TW9 1SR*

© Marion Lennox 1996

ISBN 0 263 79803 8

*Set in Times 10 on 10 pt. by
Rowland Phototypesetting Limited
Bury St Edmunds, Suffolk*

03-9609-52639

Made and printed in Great Britain

CHAPTER ONE

TRESPASSERS WILL BE SHOT.

The sign was huge. It almost covered the farm gate and, not surprisingly, it made Jessica pause.

She didn't pause for long.

Dr Jessie Harvey stared down at the pathetic drag marks leading to the gap beside the gate. Harry must have dragged himself through—and there were traces of blood on the path.

Sign or no sign, there was no choice. Jess had to look.

Niall Mountmarche might have half the island scared silly with his stupid signs but if Harry was suffering somewhere on the other side of the fence. . .

Sod Niall Mountmarche's sign!

Jessica Harvey, Barega Island's only veterinary surgeon, pushed stray wisps of soft brown curls from her angry eyes and pushed open the gate.

She'd been here before and she hadn't been shot.

Louis Mountmarche, wine-maker extraordinaire, had been the island children's ogre for years. Rumour said that he'd shot a child in the dim, distant past and his reputation was fearsome.

By the time Jess had arrived to work on the island the old man was hardly ever seen by the locals.

Four months ago the local police had asked Jess to investigate reports of animal cruelty. Neighbours had complained that the old man's dog had been howling for days.

She'd found the dog.

The neighbours had been right. The animal had been neglected but it hadn't been the old man's fault. When Jessie and the police had finally found him, Louis Mountmarche had been dead for weeks—with his dog guarding his body.

5

Although the fate of the old man and his dog had shocked the locals, the islanders hadn't blamed themselves. The old man had abused everyone—and now it seemed that his nephew was of the same mould.

Niall Mountmarche, nephew of Louis, had arrived on the island three months ago by private boat and his contact with the locals since then had been restricted to necessary business. The threatening signs had been renewed.

It seemed that there was a family trait of isolation and aggression.

The ogre reputation was building again among the local children and the unknown Niall Mountmarche did nothing to refute it.

So. . .

So Jessie shouldn't be here, crawling on all fours between the grapevines trying desperately to follow the broken trail of drag marks and blood.

The ground had been recently furrowed. It was early spring on the island and the vines were just budding. Someone had been here recently, ploughing weeds into the ground and, by the smell of the rich loam, applying fertilizer.

'Harry,' Jessie called softly.

Drat the Mountmarches. They had her spooked. She took a deep breath and rose to her feet. The trail ended here but where the vines were still bare she'd surely see an injured dog if it was in the open.

Jessie raised her voice. 'Harry!'

There was no response.

Or was there? Had she heard something?

Jessie's face turned in the morning sun toward a bank of trees further down the slope. In the trees there was cover—and an injured dog would head for cover if it possibly could. The sound—if she hadn't imagined it—had come from there.

She was too close to the Mountmarche house for comfort. For a moment Jessie considered approaching the house to ask permission to search—but only for a moment. The Mountmarche reputation suggested that she'd be marched off the property at the point of a gun—and where would that leave Harry?

'Harry?' Jess called again, lowering her voice and heading down the slopes into the cover of the trees. She cast a nervous glance at the house and her voice dropped even further. 'Harry!'

A pathetic whimper cut across the silence, so low that she would have missed it if her ears hadn't been straining to hear.

He was here. Somewhere.

Here, where the ground was rough and overgrown and the banks of a creek fell away from the fertile soil, there were hundreds of places that a wounded dog could crawl to die.

She could hear him clearly now. His whimpers increased as she called him.

The branches were thick over her head, barring her path. Swearing softly to herself, Jessie slung her bag over her shoulder and dropped to the ground again.

She'd have to crawl.

Her knees were bare and the twigs and branches littering the ground dug into them—but if she stood up she wouldn't be able to see. She'd have no hope of finding him.

'Harry,' she called again. 'Harry. . .'

Jessie pushed her nose through a thicket of undergrowth and stopped dead.

A pair of black boots blocked her path.

And a gun.

Jessie practically yelped in fright. She jumped about a foot and when she finally came down to earth her heart was thumping like a battering ram.

The island children had done their job well. The Ogre of Barega had been built up to such a fearsome figure that it was all Jessie could do not to scramble to her feet and run.

Instead, she forced herself to squat back on her heels and look up.

It was hardly a position of dignity. To be caught crawling on all fours on someone else's land was scarcely a desirable fate at the best of times—but to be caught by a Mountmarche. . .

Niall Mountmarche. . .

Ogre of Barega. . .

Jessie's first impression was of size—and of darkness. The man wore black knee-length boots over dark riding jodhpurs, and a black short-sleeved shirt open almost to the waist. The wind-tossed hair around the man's lean, harsh face was jet black as well and his angry eyes were as dark as night.

The Ogre was in his mid-thirties, Jessie guessed.

The Mountmarche she'd seen—old Louis—had been short and stout but Jess saw no similarity between Louis and his nephew. This man was over six feet tall and hadn't an ounce of spare flesh on his strongly built body.

Or compassion, Jessie guessed, as she slowly rose to a standing position. Niall Mountmarche's face was flint hard, repellent with anger.

Even as she found her feet and stood before him, he still made her feel tiny.

And scared stiff.

The man's hands were gripping his gun as though he'd love to use it. He wasn't pointing the thing at her—but it didn't make it one whit less threatening.

'G-good morning,' she stammered.

The Ogre of Barega was looking at the girl before him as though she was a repugnant form of insect life. Jessie flushed in mortification. His look was nothing short of contemptuous.

Well, Niall Mountmarche wasn't to know that Jessie was the island's vet. She hardly looked professional, she thought grimly. The young vet was wearing shorts and sneakers; her knees were dust-caked from crawling along the furrowed ground and her face was probably the same. Her shoulder-length curls had caught on briars and were tangled and wild.

Niall Mountmarche didn't know why Jess was on his land. Maybe he was right to look like this—when she was so clearly trespassing.

Jess pushed her tangled curls back with a defiant flourish—and felt more dirt streak down her cheek as Niall Mountmarche finally spoke.

'What the hell are you doing on my land?' The man's voice was deep and resonant with a trace of an accent she couldn't quite place—and more than a trace of anger.

It was hardly a promising start.

Jessie bit her lip and forced herself to hold out her hand in an attempt at greeting.

'Hi,' she said unsteadily. 'I'm. . .I'm Jessica Harvey. . .'

'I'm not the least bit interested in who you are,' the man snapped. His dark eyes flashed his displeasure. 'The sign on my gate is there for a purpose—and it means what it says. This is no place for teenagers to play stupid games—so I suggest you get yourself off my land now.'

Teenagers. . .

Jessie's flush faded. Teenagers. . . How old did he take her for, for heaven's sake? She drew herself up to her full five feet five inches and her brown eyes glared.

'I'm twenty-seven,' she snapped.

He shrugged. 'Fascinating, I'm sure.' The man's cold gaze raked Jessie's slim form, from her filthy sneakers to her dust-caked face. His disdain only seemed to increase. 'If you're speaking the truth—' his tone suggested such a thing was as plausible as the moon being made of cheese '—then I suggest you're too old to be crawling round my property on what, I must assume, to be some sort of infantile game. Now collect this Harry—or whoever it is you're calling—and get the hell out of here. Now!'

Harry. . .

'Harry's a dog,' Jessie managed.

'You brought dogs onto my property?' The man

looked as if he was preparing to explode in fury. His fingers whitened on the gun and Jessie blenched. What on earth had she got herself into?

'I didn't bring him. . . He's not my dog and I can't find him,' she stammered, striving desperately for calm.

The man visibly fought for self-control. His leather-booted foot stirred the ground, like a bull before a charge, and his face was cold as ice.

'So you didn't bring him? He's not your dog but you're looking for him,' he said coldly. 'I see.' He raised his gun slightly. 'Then I suggest you leave my land now—and let me do the looking.'

The gun's slight movement was so suggestive that Jessie blenched. He wouldn't shoot Harry. . .

'No!'

Instinctively Jessie's hand reached out to the gun and held on hard. She pulled it towards herself, swinging the point away from her body.

The man didn't release it. He stood like stone, immovable.

'Are you playing games with me?' the man said slowly. The foot had stopped its movement. He stood rigidly, his hand locked on the gun and his cold eyes staring down at her. Jessie had never felt such anger—such a blaze of hostility. . .

Or had she. . .?

Once. . .

A wave of such dreadful remembrance hit her that Jessie stepped back in horror. Her hands dropped from the gun as if burned.

Jessie's face drained of what little colour she had left and instinctively her hands came up before her face—to ward off a blow. . .

It was a futile gesture. This man hadn't threatened her with a gun—or with a raised hand for that matter—but the fury was there. . .

And suddenly it wasn't.

The man's face changed. The aggression died as he

stared down at her and his hand came out as if to touch. . .

Jess stepped back in panic. 'N-no. . .'

'I won't hurt you,' he said harshly.

There was a long silence. The morning sun glimmered through the canopy of leaves above them. Their eyes stayed locked, the man's harsh stare changing to a look of confusion—as if, suddenly, his aggression was weakening.

Jessie's fear remained.

How could it not?

The man swore suddenly. He took another step towards her and Jessie flinched again.

He stopped.

And swore again.

And, then, in a gesture of impatience the man broke the barrel of his gun. The cartridge fell out onto his palm and he let it fall further onto the ground. Then he let the gun fall, too.

'I won't hurt you,' he said again and this time he spoke as though he meant it. The blazing anger was gone.

Jessie took a deep breath. The memory receded—a little. This man wasn't John Talbot. He had no cause to hurt her.

'I. . .I guess. . .' she said, but she couldn't make her voice steady.

'Are you running from someone?' Niall Mountmarche's dark brow was creased in sudden concern. Clearly her reaction had him puzzled. He looked around as if expecting to see others. 'Are you hiding? Who's Harry?'

'I told you—Harry's a dog.' It was all Jessie could do to get her voice above a whisper.

'But not your dog?'

'No.'

'But you're scared stiff?'

Jessie took a deep breath. 'No. Not. . .not any more.'

'Because I put the gun down.'

'That might have something to do with it,' Jessie stammered, her equilibrium returning by degrees. The man still unsettled her badly—but at least the ogre image was fading. For the moment. . .

'Well, would you care to tell me?'

'Yes.' Jessie closed her eyes, still fighting for calm. When she opened them she had herself almost under control.

'Harry is your neighbour's dog,' she said at last. 'Frank Reid owns land on your north boundary. I guess you don't know him—as you keep to yourself so much—but Frank is elderly and diabetic. He's ill at the moment and has been in hospital for over a week.'

'So?' This was of supreme disinterest, Niall Mountmarche's face told her.

'The girl who's been looking after his farm told Frank today that Harry's been missing for almost a week,' Jess stammered. 'Frank asked me to look. . .'

'A week. . .'

'She didn't want to worry him.' Jessie's voice trailed away. The girl's actions were almost inexcusable, she thought, remembering the elderly farmer's distress when she'd seen him that morning.

'So he asked you to look because you're a friend?' Niall Mountmarche was watching her as if she was a specimen he just couldn't make out.

'Because I'm the island vet,' Jessie said bluntly and watched his reaction.

It was all she could have hoped for.

The man's eyes widened in incredulity—and then disbelief.

'I don't believe it,' he said flatly.

'That's fine.' Jessie bit her lip and shrugged. 'Just let me get on with finding the dog and there's no need for you to believe anything.'

'How long have you been qualified?'

'Look!' Jessie's voice exploded into anger. 'How long I've been qualified has nothing to do with anything. The only thing that matters at the moment is that there's an injured dog on your property and I need to find him. Fast!'

Niall Mountmarche was still watching her—assessing her. With his eyes still on her, he stooped to pick up his gun and snap it together. As Jessie's face changed again he flicked the cartridge with his booted toe so that it lay almost at her feet.

'You keep the cartridge,' he said harshly. 'I won't shoot your precious dog. But I want to know why you think he's on my property.'

The air whooshed out of Jessie's lungs in a rush. She stooped to retrieve the cartridge and shoved it deep into her pocket—before the man changed his mind.

'There are rabbit traps set near your boundary fence,' she told him, fingering the cartridge as security. 'Some of the local kids must have set their traps on Frank's land while he's in hospital. They know he'd never let them, otherwise. The traps are set in a pattern and one trap seems to be missing—and the place where it should be is marked with blood and fur. Not brown rabbit fur. It's the black and white fur of a collie.'

'Collie?'

'Harry—Frank's dog—is a Border collie. A good one.'

He was certainly a lovely dog, Jessie knew, and if anything happened to Harry Frank Reid would break his heart.

'You haven't said why you believe he's here.' The booted toe was tapping again on the leaf-strewn ground. Patience, it seemed, was not one of Niall Mountmarche's strong points.

'There's a trail of drag marks and blood leading through your fence. At a guess, the dog still has the trap on his foot. If he's too injured to drag himself home then he won't have gone far.'

'If he's been missing a week then he'll be dead.'

'No.' Jessie shook her head. 'I heard him,' she said flatly. 'He's somewhere here.'

The man's eyes narrowed. 'Nearby?'

'Yes.'

'Well, what are we wasting time for, Jessica Harvey?' the man demanded harshly. 'Let's find him.'

'You mean. . . You mean you'll help?'

'Why on earth wouldn't I?'

Why not, indeed?

It took fifteen minutes.

At the sound of Niall's voice Harry's whimpers had ceased and, no matter how much Jessie called, she wasn't able to hear the dog again. Then it was a case of physically searching inside every hollow log and under every piece of undergrowth.

In the end it wasn't Niall who found Harry but Harry who found Niall. Niall lifted a piece of bush and Harry's black face lunged forward in snarling menace. Teeth sank into Niall's leather boot—and then the dog shrieked in pain as his movement made the agony from his injuries unbearable. The dog fell back, teeth still bared in a grimace of suffering.

Jessie had heard. She came flying from twenty yards away, half expecting Niall Mountmarche to kick out in fury.

The Ogre of Barega did no such thing. The man knelt, just out of range of the menacing teeth, and his voice softened.

'Hey, old fella,' he said gently. 'We've been looking for you. There's no need to attack. We're here to help.'

He knew animals, then. Jessie's fears receded further. This man knew a desperately injured dog would react by defending itself. The worse its pain became the more it would defend itself—to the point where a badly injured dog could even bite its owner.

Harry was confused and in pain and, Jessie guessed, starved almost to death. They could expect no co-operation from Harry.

Jess knelt beside Niall and looked under the bush where Harry lay. All she could see were the whites of his eyes wide with terror—and the bared teeth.

'Any suggestions?' Niall asked and his tone was sardonic again. It suggested that Jessie's claim to being a vet was ridiculous.

'I'll dart him with a tranquilliser if I must,' Jessie said, hauling her bag from her shoulder and flicking it open. 'But I don't want to. He'll be weak enough as it is.'

'So, what. . .?'

Jessie lifted her tray of syringes and dressings from the top of the bag and found what she was looking for. A leather muzzle. Normally she could manage without—if she could reach the dog from behind—but Harry was wedged firmly into his hiding place and could only be faced head-on. To put her hands into his refuge was to risk losing a finger.

'OK.' She looked back at the collie. The big dog hadn't moved. The teeth were still drawn back in a grimace half of pain, half of menace.

'No sudden movements,' she said shortly.

Niall nodded. He didn't move.

'OK, Harry,' Jess said gently, turning her full attention on the dog. 'Let's help you. Come on, boy. We're here to help.'

She talked for five minutes, taking all the time in the world. The dog had hurt himself by his lunge forward and Jess was prepared to wait for the agony to settle. She needed the terror to recede from those huge, pain-filled eyes.

She knew this dog. Frank Reid was a friend and Jess saw Harry often when she dropped in to Frank's farm. She'd removed a burr from his ear last summer and he'd let her help as soon as she had his trust.

This time he was more desperately hurt. It would take time—but she could afford to take it.

'Come on, Harry,' she said gently. 'We're here to help. You can trust us.'

Inch by inch she edged forward, her eyes never leaving the dog's for a moment. Beside her, Niall Mountmarche watched and listened—but didn't move either. He sensed that he could destroy all her efforts with a movement. At least the man had the rudiments of common sense.

Jessie held the muzzle forward, letting the dog see it. He hadn't seen such a thing before—so he didn't know it wasn't to be trusted. Jess let it lie like a hand-kerchief in her hand, holding it forward.

'Hey, Harry. . .'

An inch more. . . An inch more. . .

The dog's lips moved. His body shuddered and he lunged forward, desperately defending. . .

Right into the muzzle.

Jessie moved like lightning. She was up over the big dog, fastening the leather thong at the back of his neck and then hauling the dog from his hiding place and gathering the collie to her like a frightened child. She held him immobile and rigid against her, pulling him down to her and talking and talking as if there was absolutely no threat. . .

The dog could do nothing.

Normally Jess would have to fight for control of a big dog but, muzzled, Harry was helpless.

He sagged against Jess and the fight left him. The collie lay limply on her knee and the huge eyes looked up pleadingly.

I don't know what to do, the eyes seemed to say. Help me.

'Hey, Harry. . .'

The dog whimpered in pain.

There was no longer a threat from those razor-sharp teeth so Jess removed the muzzle. Now that Harry was in the open she could control him and the muzzle would only distress him more than he already was.

Jess put her hand on the big dog's matted coat and felt the beginnings of tears prick behind her eyes as she saw the extent of his injuries.

There was little she could do here—except put the dog out of his misery.

The trap was still in place, cruelly cutting the foot

between wrist and toe. The wound on the dog's leg had turned into a festering mess. The tissue was necrotic, Jess thought grimly, her nose wrinkling at the unmistakable smell. She could see bone—the metacarpals—through the torn flesh. They must be broken.

Heaven knew how the dog had managed to get this far with the trap still cutting into him—and heaven knew how he'd survived this long with a wound like this.

'Oh, Harry. . .'

She stroked the dog's head with a hand that trembled and then took a deep breath. Emotion would help nothing. What had to be done should be done quickly.

'Hand me my bag,' she told Niall Mountmarche as she came to her hard decision—but the tremor in her voice was unmistakable.

'What will you do?' Niall Mountmarche was looking down at the dog's leg and the expression on his face was pretty much how Jess was feeling. Sick.

'Put him down.'

Niall's face swung from dog to girl.

'I thought you said the dog wasn't yours?' he demanded.

'He's not. Could I have my bag, please?'

Niall didn't move. He looked back to the dog's leg. 'Doesn't the owner have the cash or inclination to pay for your services then, Dr Harvey?'

The emphasis on the word 'Doctor' was almost a sneer.

Jessie flushed.

'I can't operate,' she said stiffly.

'But you said you were a vet.'

'Yes. I'm a vet. And I need to stop Harry suffering even more. Could you pass the bag, please?'

'But you could operate.' Gently Niall Mountmarche moved forward and lifted the dog's leg from where it lay across Jessie's bare knee. The dog hardly stirred. Niall examined the leg with caution, touching the pad with infinite care.

'There's warmth in his pad,' he told Jessie. 'There's still some circulation. I don't think he'd even have to lose his leg. Once we get the trap off. . .'

'I don't think you understand,' Jessie said flatly. 'I haven't the facilities to operate.'

'But you are a qualified vet?'

'Yes.'

Niall's face stilled. 'Then you'll be the vet who put my uncle's dog down. The easy way out——is that it, Dr Harvey? You didn't wait for my permission before killing my uncle's dog.'

Jess closed her eyes. Her hands still stroked the dog's matted fur and she fought to keep her voice calm so as not to frighten Harry even more.

'Your uncle's dog was an old, old Dobermann,' she said softly, trying not to look up at those accusing eyes. 'He'd been trained to attack to kill anything and anybody who wasn't his owner. He was starving and near death when we found him; he had some sort of arthritic debility in his back legs and even if I'd saved him he was too old to form a bond with a new owner.

'Maybe. . .maybe if you'd been in closer contact with your uncle——if I could have found you quickly—— but as it was we didn't know Louis Mountmarche had a living relative. . .'

'Are you saying it's my fault the dog had to die?'

'I'm saying, given that there was no owner, I had no choice,' Jessie snapped. 'As I have no choice now.'

'But this dog has an owner and he's younger.' Niall's attention had changed focus again——from anger back to concentration. He bent over the wounded pad and examined it with care, seemingly not repulsed by the stinking flesh. 'How old, Dr Harvey?'

'He's only three,' Jessie said sadly. She shook her head. 'I know. . . Given different circumstances. . .'

'What different circumstances?'

'An assistant who can given an anaesthetic.' Jessie sighed. 'You're right. Maybe——maybe if I could put him under an anaesthetic and clean up the mess then he'd have a chance. But he's in dreadful condition. It's going to take me ages to set the bones and clean up the mess.

'He won't tolerate the intravenous anaesthetic I can give myself—and there's no way I can operate on a dog as sick as this and intubate at the same time. Intubating and operating by yourself is like drunk driving—OK if conditions are perfect and nothing goes wrong. But there are already major things going wrong here. So. . .I think it's kinder to acknowledge defeat now.'

Niall Mountmarche's dark brow snapped down. 'Don't you have a trained vet nurse?'

'This is a tiny island,' Jessie told him. 'What I really need is another vet—but, no, I don't even have a trained nurse.'

'But. . .' Niall's fingers had moved to fondle the dog's soft ears. The big collie seemed almost unconscious. He'd gone past fear. He lay, passive and trusting, and Jessie's heart went out to the magnificent animal. 'What about the island human medical services? Surely there's a doctor and nurses on the island who could help out?'

'There are.' Jessie's face set. 'But the nurses haven't the training to give anaesthetic. And the doctor won't.'

'"Won't"?'

Niall echoed the word blankly and it hung between them in the soft morning sunshine. A question. . .

'"Won't",' Jessie repeated. She held out her hand in silent demand. 'Please. . . Could you pass me my bag?'

Niall Mountmarche ignored her. 'What do you mean, "won't"?'

Jess sighed. 'The island's two trained doctors—a husband-and-wife team—are away for twelve months doing further training on the mainland. The locum replacing them had to leave because of family problems and the present locum—well, Lionel Hurd won't touch animals. He says it's not in his contract and he's right.' She sighed again. 'I can't force him.'

'So Harry dies.'

'So Harry dies,' Jess said sadly. She looked up at Niall then and met those dark, angry eyes full-on. 'Unless you have any other suggestions, Mr Mountmarche?'

There was a long, long silence.

'Hand me my bag,' Jess said finally again into the stillness—but Niall Mountmarche shook his head.

He touched the injured dog's leg once more and gentle fingers carefully probed the rotten flesh. His touch was so gentle that the dog didn't so much as flinch.

Finally Niall nodded, as if coming to a hard decision.

'I do have an alternative suggestion,' he told Jess, his voice firming as he spoke.

'Which is?' Jessie sounded sceptical, she knew. Her voice was flat and hopeless—but she loved this dog.

'I'll give the anaesthetic.'

'You!'

He shrugged. 'I can do it.'

'But how. . .?' Jess looked down at those long, sensitive fingers, skilfully and gently examining the wound. 'You're not. . .'

'A vet? No.' He shook his head. 'I'm not. So you're going to have to talk me through it, Dr Harvey. But I do have medical skills. I'm a doctor.'

CHAPTER TWO

A DOCTOR. . .

Jessie's jaw sagged. It took a real effort to haul her mouth closed again.

'I don't believe. . .' she started and then, at the look on Niall Mountmarche's face, she stopped.

He hadn't believed that she was a vet—and now she was showing the same distrust.

A doctor. . .

From Ogre of Barega to medical doctor—like Dr Jekyll and Mr Hyde. . .

'What. . .what sort of a doctor?' she asked cautiously, and for the first time she saw a glimmer of a smile touch Niall Mountmarche's face.

'Not a doctor of philosophy,' he reassured her. 'Or of basket-weaving, for that matter. A people doctor. Doctor of medicine with a piece of paper from London University to prove it.'

'An English doctor!'

'I'll confess I'm an English doctor,' he agreed. 'Does that make me less qualified?' The smile deepened. 'You colonials really are getting uppity.' Then Niall looked down at the dog on Jessie's lap and the smile faded. 'Enough. We're wasting time. Let's get this trap off and move him. Is your car near the gate on the ridge?'

'Yes.' Jessie's mind was working at a hundred miles an hour. 'But. . .'

'But what?' Niall had risen and was standing over girl and dog, looking down. 'Now what, Dr Harvey?'

'You really are a doctor. . .?'

'I really am.' Once more that glimmer of a smile. The Ogre took a giant step back, to be replaced by someone altogether more human.

21

'Then. . .' Jessie hesitated. 'My car is fifteen minutes' walk—more if we're carrying Harry without jolting him. I don't want to remove the trap until I have Harry under anaesthetic. It may bleed like crazy and I'll have to work fast. But I don't want him carried far with the trap in place. Do you have a car at your home?'

'Yes.' His face had lost expression.

'Then can we take him to your place?'

'You mean you want me to drive him to your clinic? Is that what you're suggesting?'

Jessie took a deep breath. She glanced down at Harry and the very limpness of his body strengthened her resolution. The Mountmarche house—and Niall Mountmarche's car—was a few minutes' walk away. Taking Harry to Jessie's car meant a rough fifteen minute walk with the trap in place—or taking the trap off now and risking further bleeding.

And if Niall Mountmarche could give the anaesthetic then the dog had a chance!

'Yes,' she said firmly. 'If we carry him together then we can move him with little jolting to the pad.'

Niall's smile had faded once more, gone as if it had never been. 'I don't like strangers at my house,' he said shortly, and Jessie flinched at the coldness of his words.

Back cometh the ogre. . .

'I thought I introduced myself,' she made herself say, replacing his smile with one of her own. 'That makes me not a stranger, Dr Niall Mountmarche.'

She was fighting here. For Harry. . .

For a moment she expected a stinging rebuff. He wanted to give her one—she could tell.

Then Niall looked down again at the dog in Jessie's arms and his look softened. If he was fighting a war then he was losing. Somewhere inside was a soft core.

'I guess you're not,' he said slowly and in his voice was a small note of discovery. 'Well, Dr Harvey. If you're not a stranger then I suggest you act like a medical colleague. And we've got a job to do. So let's get on with it.'

He stooped and took the dog from her as though the creature was weightless and, as Jessie supported the trapped pad, Niall swung Harry gently up to lie cradled against his body.

The impression of a man of compassion was stirring and beginning to grow. Jessie looked up at man and dog—and there was something else stirring within that she didn't want to think about.

Niall Mountmarche met her look and his eyes widened.

It was as if he'd read her thoughts.

As if there was some sort of communication channel between them that needed no words. That was beyond words. . .

She was being ridiculous.

With a mammoth effort Jessie tore her eyes away, made sure Niall's hand was supporting the injured pad and then turned to find her bag.

'Let. . .let's go, then, Dr Mountmarche,' she said unsteadily and fumbled in the undergrowth for her belongings.

'Let's go,' Niall Mountmarche repeated and by his words Jessie knew that she wasn't imagining it.

Whatever she was feeling, Niall Mountmarche was feeling it too.

They didn't talk on the walk to the house.

Jessie walked swiftly beside Niall, struggling to keep up with his long strides, support the trap and watch the big dog's pain-dulled eyes at the same time. He was so far gone. At any moment she expected to see those big eyes glaze over. . .

The Mountmarche house was three minutes' walk along the creek bed. It was a ramshackle old homestead, grand in its day but long fallen into disrepair. Jessie had expected the house to be deserted but as they neared the house she stared in astonishment as a man emerged from the back door.

The man was elderly, wiry and wrinkled to almost

prune-like appearance. He looked like a man who'd spent his life in the sun. Like he'd been dried in the sun. . .

'What the. . .?' The elderly man stopped short as he caught sight of the group emerging from the bushland. His hand rose to scratch his bald head in a gesture of bewilderment. 'What've you got there, Doc?'

Doc. . . So Niall really was. . .

'An injured dog,' Niall said brusquely. He motioned with his head to Jessie by his side. 'Hugo, this is Jessica Harvey, the local vet. The dog's been caught in a trap, Hugo. Can you bring the Range Rover round before Paige sees us?'

She'd already seen. There was someone else emerging from the house behind Hugo.

'Daddy. . .' The word was a cry of shock.

Niall's face changed. He faced the door of the house like a man expecting trouble.

'Paige. . .'

A tiny, elfin-like creature was limping into the doorway.

She was maybe five or six—no more—with a body that was thin to the point of malnourishment. The child's white-gold hair was tied with a red ribbon that only added to her paleness and her eyes were huge in her pinched, wan face.

The little girl's body swayed a little as though she was unused to the crutches she was using for support. Both her stick-like legs were encased in callipers— iron frames that seemed too big for her tiny body.

'Daddy. . .' It was both an accusation and a cry of pain and Jessie saw Niall Mountmarche flinch like a man struck.

Silence stretched out. There was something going on here that Jessie had no idea of.

All she could do was to stand and wait.

And watch. . .

Finally, Niall seemed to come to a decision. He gently moved Harry in his arms so that he and not

Jessie was supporting the injured pad. Then he carried the dog over to where Paige stood, stooping so that the child could see the injured animal.

'Paige, I know I promised you no one would come,' Niall said softly, and his voice reminded Jessie of the tone she used with wild creatures. 'I promised it would be just you and Hugo and I. But this is Harry. He's a three-year-old Border collie and his leg's been caught in a rabbit trap. You can see that he's dreadfully hurt.

'Now, this lady is Dr Harvey and she's the local vet. She's been searching for Harry. If it's OK with you I'm going to drive Dr Harvey and Harry down to the veterinary clinic and help her operate on Harry—but if I keep my promise to you and keep us completely to ourselves then I can't help and Harry might die. It's up to you, Paige.'

What on earth was he doing? Jessie looked from man to child in bewilderment.

The child was obviously almost as confused as Jessie. She looked from Jessie to the dog in her father's arms and then back to Jessie. Her eyes didn't trust Jessie one inch.

'She's. . .she's a dog doctor?' The voice was trembling.

'Dr Harvey's a dog doctor.'

The little girl looked down at Harry and her hand went out in involuntary compassion.

'He's. . . The doggie's hurting.'

'Yes, Paige,' Niall told her, still in that low, gentle tone, as if expecting the child to turn and run. 'He's hurting badly. You can see that.'

'And. . .and you can help the lady doctor make the dog better.'

'You know I'm a doctor, too, Paige,' Niall said gently. 'It's my job. If you agree.'

The child touched the dog's soft ears.

'He really could die?'

'He really could die.'

The little girl sighed—the sigh of someone letting

something precious go out of sight and not knowing if
she'd ever see it again——but willing to take the risk.
For something as priceless as the life of this dog.

'You'll be longer than when you go to the shops?'
'Much longer, Paige. But Hugo will still be here.'
'OK,' Paige whispered. 'But. . . But hurry back. . .'

The drive to the clinic was in near-silence. Jessie sat on
the passenger side of Niall Mountmarche's gleaming
Range Rover with the dog cradled against her and let
a thousand questions crowd through her mind as
Niall drove.

There were answers to none of them.

The dog whimpered and stirred in her arms and
Jessie's hold on him tightened.

'Soon,' she whispered to the big collie.

It couldn't be soon enough for Harry.

They operated on Harry fifteen minutes later.

'Instructions, please,' Niall said briefly as they
carried the dog into Theatre.

Niall listened with care as Jess outlined the anaesthetic procedure. It wasn't so different from human
intubation. Niall flung fast questions at her and Jess
began to relax as she responded. She not only had a
skilled doctor here. In Niall Mountmarche, Jess had
found someone who was prepared to learn and
learn fast.

There was minimal delay.

As soon as the anaesthetic took effect the dreadful
trap was removed, allowing Jessie to see what she was
facing.

It was bad——but it could have been worse.

Swiftly, moving as a team with this strange new
doctor, Jessie staunched the blood flow and X-rayed.
Three of the metacarpals were fractured which meant
that she'd have to fix the bones. There was necrotic
tissue on the front of the pad and up the dog's foreleg,

as though infection had spread, but Niall was right. There was still circulation.

There was still hope.

Niall Mountmarche intubated the dog with skill, moving his obvious skills with human anaesthesia to the animal arena with thoughtfulness and intelligence. The questions he needed to know he asked before Jessie thought of telling him and she was left alone to concentrate on the wound.

It was enough.

She never could have coped with such a severely traumatised dog and vicious wound if she'd had to do the anaesthetic herself. Over and over in her head as she operated Jessie was offering silent prayers of thankfulness for this man's arrival.

The dog would be dead without him.

It was a nasty piece of surgery, requiring all her skill.

The rotten flesh had to be cut away and dirt, grass and hay seeds carefully cleaned from the festering wound. It was a time-consuming task, made more difficult by the small number of blood vessels remaining viable.

Then the metacarpals had to be fixed into position with K-wire. If only one of the outer metacarpals had been broken Jess could have let it be but with three fractured the dog would lose function if they weren't fixed.

A huge job. . .

Jess could amputate if she had to—but the shock of such radical surgery could be enough to kill an already weakened, frail animal. Even taking the trap from his foot without an anaesthetic might have been enough to send him over the edge.

At least the pad still had circulation because, miraculously, the rotten flesh hadn't invaded the major blood vessels. Yet. . . Another half a day and it would have been too late.

Too late for both the leg and for Harry, Jessie thought grimly as she worked. He would have been dead from starvation and infection.

Not now. . . Please. . . If they gave him maximum dose antibiotic and intravenous fluid to rehydrate the body. . .

Niall Mountmarche had given the dog a chance at life. She had to be grateful.

Niall. . .

Even though her whole concentration was needed for the job in hand, Jessie couldn't help being aware of the man working silently by her side. He was watching everything she did, she knew, and the thought, instead of making her feel nervous, in fact steadied her.

What on earth was such a man doing in a place like this? Growing wine? The thought seemed ridiculous and yet only hours ago the thought of him being a doctor had seemed ridiculous. And what was wrong with the little girl?

Such questions had to be put aside until later. . . Much later.

Finally, she'd done all she could. Carefully she dressed the wound and moved to help Niall reverse the anaesthetic.

Now. . .

Now it was up to Harry.

Jess smiled as she finally stepped back from the table and stripped off her gloves. 'Thank you, Dr Mountmarche,' she said simply. Her face was showing more exhaustion than she knew.

'It's the least I can do,' Niall Mountmarche told her brusquely. He'd adjusted the antibiotic through the intravenous drip and was now looking at Jess as if he couldn't really believe what he was seeing. 'That was a fine piece of work, Dr Harvey. I'm sorry I doubted your qualifications.'

Jessie stared. An apology from the Ogre of Barega. What next?

'You don't make such a bad vet yourself,' she smiled at him. 'For a human doctor.'

For a human doctor. . .

All of a sudden he was. Immensely human.

And immensely male.

He smiled then, his smile reflecting her relief, and
Jess felt her heart give an unexpected jolt. What a
smile. . .

Crazy. . .

She turned swiftly to the sink before her colour
began to rise.

Or maybe it already had.

Maybe it was too late to disguise what she was
feeling.

Niall Mountmarche was watching her with a look
that she didn't understand in the least. It made her
feel. . .

Vulnerable.

And slightly afraid.

She struggled with the tapes of her gown and Niall
moved swiftly to release them. The gown was lifted
away, revealing once more her dust-stained shorts and
shirt and bare arms and legs.

'Back to Jessica Harvey, adolescent in need of a good
bath,' Niall grinned, and Jessie was forced to smile.

'It's hard being clinically clean when you're a vet.'

'There are not a lot of vets I know who crawl round
under grapevines looking for patients.' Niall motioned
to Harry. 'Will you leave him here?'

'I'll take him into the kitchen,' Jessie told him. 'It's
warm by the stove and I can watch him recover and
make myself lunch at the same time.' She hesitated
and glanced at her watch. It was almost two in the
afternoon. 'Would you. . .would you like some lunch?'

'No. I have to get back.'

Back to being the Ogre of Barega. Back to Paige.

'Please. . .' Jess put out a hand and laid it on his bare
arm—and then wished she hadn't. The feel of his skin
against her fingers did something odd to her legs.

She lifted the hand away but made herself repeat
the word.

'Please. . . Before you go. Come and see Frank with

me. He's the owner of the dog and he's here in the same building——only over the other side.'

'Yes, I heard you had twin animal and human hospitals,' Niall grinned. 'A Health Department nightmare.'

'What the heart doesn't know. . .' Jessie said demurely and matched his grin. 'We're a long way from officialdom here, thank heaven, and the arrangements have worked well until now.'

'And now?'

'Dr Hurd doesn't like my animals.' Jessie shrugged. 'It doesn't matter. We can be very separate when we try. Will you come and see Frank?'

He glanced at his watch. 'Paige will be waiting. . .' Then he looked up at Jess and smiled, that heart-warming, heart-stopping smile that was all the things that Jess considered most dangerous in a man.

'Ten minutes, Dr Harvey,' he smiled. 'Ten minutes more of human contact before I go back to being the Ogre of Barega.'

He knew. He knew of his reputation.

Jessie felt herself flush crimson but Niall Mountmarche was smiling in a way that showed he didn't mind the title in the least——in fact, by the look of it, he rather liked it!

They wheeled Harry down to the kitchen and settled him into a cage beside the big slow combustion stove. Jess worked with swift efficiency but Niall Mountmarche stopped at the kitchen door and stared in amazement.

'Good grief!'

'What?' Jess was lifting the dog from trolley to cage, careful not to tangle his intravenous line, and Niall recovered from shock enough to move to help her.

'It's hardly a clinically clean kitchen——pristine for cooking,' Niall told her. He hooked the bag of saline above the cage.

'It's clean enough for me.'

Niall shook his head. Having settled the dog, he stood and stared around the room.

It certainly was unusual. The house had been built with mass entertaining in mind and now, even though it was separated into two wings—hospital and vet clinic—Jess had been able to keep the original kitchen for her own use. She used every inch of it.

The vast slow combustion stove was the kitchen's heart but surrounding it was ordered jumble. Bags of animal formula were heaped along one wall; there were tiny woollen bags with heating pads—obviously used for injured wildlife—hanging from chairs and, above their heads, bunches and bunches of sweet-smelling lavender hung like fragrant clouds.

'You eat your cornflakes in here?' Niall demanded incredulously and Jessie smiled. Her fingers were smoothing Harry's soft ears, settling him from anaesthetic to deep, natural sleep. The longer he slept now the better. He wouldn't worry the intravenous line and she could get maximum fluid and antibiotic into his starving body.

'I like it,' she said, and her voice was a little defensive. Separate your work from your home life, they'd told her at vet school, but Jess had never quite managed it.

'I think I like it too,' Niall smiled. He bent down over a woollen pouch. 'Anyone home?'

There was. A moist, pinkish-brown nose emerged, followed by two huge brown eyes. The baby wallaby checked the intruder out, cast a doubtful glance across at Jessie as much as to say, 'What are you doing letting us be disturbed when it's not dinner time?' and squirmed back down into his cocoon of wool.

'For heaven's sake. . .' Niall Mountmarche's normally grim face was transformed. He straightened and stared round the room. 'Four pouches. Are they all. . .'

'Only two are in use,' Jessie told him. 'I'm. . .I'm not taking new orphans at the moment.'

'Not taking. . .' Niall frowned. 'You mean these aren't pets?'

Jessie shook her head. 'They're wild creatures found orphaned or injured. The islanders know I care for them so they bring them to me. But I can't cope with any more than two babies without help.'

'And you're without help?'

Jessie shrugged. 'I do have a little,' she admitted. 'One of the nurses' daughters comes in for emergencies. Lucy plans to be a vet and I've taught her to prepare and give formula. Lucy fed these two this morning while I searched for Harry. But I was lucky it was a school half-holiday. Lucy goes to school and doesn't do night feeds and two-hourly feeds get a bit much when you're by yourself.'

'But you haven't always been by yourself?'

Niall Mountmarche was prowling the room, fingering equipment and formula bags as though fascinated. He threw the question at her from the other side of the room.

'My cousin and his wife are the normal island doctors and when they're here they live on the other side of the hospital,' Jessie told him. She was still absently stroking Harry but Harry was beyond feeling. Safe and warm, he was sleeping the sleep of the angels. 'They help—but without them it's difficult. For the next six months. . .'

'Oh, yes.' Niall nodded. 'For the next six months you have the horrid Lionel Hurd who doesn't like animals. I would have thought you would have written that into the job description.'

'We didn't have a choice,' Jessie said tightly. 'It was Lionel or nothing. And I guess he's better than nothing.'

'But you're not sure.'

Jessie shook her head. 'Sometimes I'm not,' she admitted, thinking of the last time that she'd had words with Lionel. The man gave her the creeps.

She pushed the thought away and crossed to the sink

to wash her hands. It was impossible to think of Lionel when Niall Mountmarche was in her kitchen. Impossible to find two such different men. . .

The feel of Niall Mountmarche in her home was sending strange sensations through Jess—sensations that she wasn't at all sure she should be encouraging. He stood looking at the domestic chaos around him and Jessie felt the weight of the past six months shift focus—as though here was someone to share her burden.

Who cared like she did. . .

Ridiculous. This was the Ogre of Barega she was thinking of—not some knight in shining armour charging into her life, stethoscope flying, to take over the medical cares of the island.

'Will you come and see Frank before you go back to Paige?' Jess asked for the second time and was aware that her words sounded abrupt. She couldn't help it. She was suddenly badly unsettled.

Niall nodded. He glanced at his watch again.

'I have five minutes,' he told her. 'Five minutes more of being a doctor before I transform again. Lead on, Dr Harvey. Whither thou goest, I will follow.'

Odd. There was a tone in his voice that suggested that he was only half joking.

Jess led the way through to the hospital side of the building with a light heart. She'd left Frank Reid desperate this morning. The elderly farmer had been beside himself when he knew that Harry had disappeared, furious with the girl who'd been caring for Harry for being afraid to tell him sooner that the dog was missing and furious with himself for not being well enough to go home.

'Danged leg,' he'd sworn, and thrown in a few more expletives besides. 'Get me a wheelchair, Jess, and I'll look for him myself.'

Only Jessie's absolute assurance that she'd search as thoroughly as Frank himself would had made him lie back on his pillows again and his face when Jess had left was of total misery. He knew what the dog's absence of almost a week most probably meant.

But now. . . Now the news that Jess could give the old man was a lot better than she could have expected. She pushed the ward door open with a smile and stopped in dismay.

Frank was in no condition to receive visitors.

The old man was vomiting. He'd been vomiting for a while, Jess could see, as he was past the stage where he was able to sit and hold the kidney basin for himself. He was dry-retching, heaving uselessly as the nurse watched helplessly beside him.

Jess stared down in dismay.

This was no normal gastric upset. Frank's eyes were sunk deep in their sockets. His skin was parchment dry and the hand clutching the coverlet was gripping convulsively.

'What's happening, Sarah?' Jess asked quickly, moving across to Frank's side. Frank was so far gone that he didn't even try to acknowledge her presence.

'I don't know.' The middle-aged nurse shook her head in indecision. 'I don't like it, Jess, and that's the truth. He's been vomiting since just after you left. He was so upset about the dog—and then he lost his breakfast and he's just kept on being sick.'

'Have you rung Dr Hurd?'

Sarah shouldn't be coping on her own here, Jessie knew. The nurse had done basic training twenty years ago but had been involved in little medicine since. She'd only just started back at the hospital after raising her family, filling in while one of the regular nurses was on holiday.

'I rang Dr Hurd twice,' the nurse whispered. 'He said to give metaclopramide—which I've done—but it's not helping. I rang him again half an hour ago and he just said to give him more. He'll be in later. . .'

Later. . .

Jess stared down at Frank and knew without doubt

that there was no 'later'. She knew what death looked like.

Dear heaven. . .

'Ring him again, then,' she said harshly. 'Tell him Mr Reid's in real trouble and he must come now!'

'He's at Clinic,' the nurse told her. 'He yelled last time when I disturbed him. He said he'd come when he was ready and not before.'

Instinctively Jess looked to Niall.

Niall Mountmarche had followed her into the room and was surveying the room with a face that was totally devoid of any expression. It was as if he was deliberately holding himself apart.

He didn't want to get involved.

'Dr Mountmarche. . .' Jess started.

'Yes?' It was a clipped, clinical reply. It could have meant anything.

'Please. . .' Jessie said helplessly and then, at the look on that cold face, she went further. 'Frank's. . . Frank's my friend. . .'

'I'm not practising medicine here, Dr Harvey— especially on someone else's patient. It's none of my business.'

'Then Frank will die.'

The words hung in the air and everyone in the room knew that they were absolute truth.

Niall looked down at the man on the bed for a long moment. Frank hadn't acknowledged their presence in any way. His frail body was heaving as if it was trying to rid itself of a poison that was overwhelming.

'Damn him,' Niall Mountmarche said savagely and Jessie knew that he wasn't talking of Frank. He was talking of the absent Lionel Hurd. He walked over to the bed and lifted the chart. 'He's diabetic, isn't he?'

'Yes.' Jessie was hardly breathing.

'What's his blood sugar?' Niall snapped at the nurse and the nurse faltered.

'B-blood sugar?'

'Blood sugar, Nurse,' Niall said and his voice was

dangerously calm. Jessie had a sudden vision of Niall in a large teaching hospital, with students behind him. The image of the Ogre of Barega was thoroughly replaced now. There was clinical calm—and clinical, icy professionalism.

'The patient is diabetic, Nurse,' Niall snapped. 'You must be doing blood-sugar readings?'

'Dr Hurd didn't tell me to. . .'

'Well, I'm telling you,' Niall snapped. 'When was the last one done? Yesterday?'

'I don't know. . . I mean. . . We give him his pills for diabetes but I didn't know we had to do blood sugars. . .'

The nurse was close to tears.

'Well, do one now, Nurse,' Niall said with that same icy calm. 'Fast.' He lifted the chart from the end of the bed. 'History. Dr Harvey, do you know it?' The nurse was already scurrying for the diabetic testing kit, sniffing back tears, and Niall had obviously given her up as a source of useful information.

'Frank was admitted to hospital a week ago with a bad leg,' Jess told him. 'It doesn't seem to be getting any better. I'm not. . . Dr Hurd doesn't discuss his treatment with me. That's all I know.'

Niall flicked up the blankets. Frank was wearing short pyjamas and his leg was exposed on the white sheet. The right leg from ankle to knee was red and swollen.

'Cellulitis,' Niall said grimly. He was holding Frank's chart in his free hand and glanced at the line of figures. Sarah had filled in temperature and blood pressure readings with neat, precise figures. It was one thing she was good at.

The nurse was taking a tiny fingerprick blood sample now for a blood-sugar reading and her hand trembled.

'He's been running a temp of over thirty-eight for seven days,' Niall said incredulously. 'There's no drip up? Has Dr Hurd discontinued intravenous anti-biotics?'

Sarah was placing the blood sample on the stick. She nearly dropped it in her fright.

'He's had antibiotics orally, Doctor,' she whispered. 'And his diabetic tablets. . .'

'So he's not on insulin?'

'Tablet only.' Sarah was sure of her ground here.

'And you haven't taken a blood-sugar reading?'

'I don't. . .' Sarah looked wildly across at Jessie. 'Maybe the night nurse did—or Dr Hurd himself—'

'Pigs might fly,' Niall snapped. He laid the chart on the bed and lifted Frank's wrist. 'I need a drip set up fast,' he told Jess. 'Can you arrange it. . .?'

'Dr Harvey's a vet,' the nurse said, shocked.

'Yes, she's a vet,' Niall growled. 'And she wouldn't treat a dog like this man's been treated. What's the blood sugar, Nurse?'

He waited.

Sarah stared at the tiny chart. It was as much as she could do to keep her hands from trembling too much to read it.

'Th-thirty-two. . .'

'Thirty-two.' Niall sighed. His voice was dangerously quiet. 'A blood sugar of sixteen should be sending danger signals. Thirty-two, and you haven't been testing. . .'

His face set into grim lines. 'Someone's been criminally negligent here,' he snapped. 'But we'll worry about that later.

'I want his urine tested for ketones as soon as possible but I won't wait on the result. He has to be suffering from diabetic ketacidosis and I'll work on that assumption. I want insulin—now—and I want saline intravenously at maximum flow. We'll also need blood for electrolytes.'

'H-how much insulin do we give him?'

'Twenty units to begin with.'

'And saline?' The nurse was practically weeping and Niall winced.

'As much as we can get aboard,' he said icily. He

was taking Frank's blood pressure as he spoke. 'Ninety on fifty. . . And you ask me how much. . .?'

'Can I help?' Jess asked quietly.

'I need equipment for an IV line. . .'

Jessie had already found it. She'd moved swiftly next door to the small theatre and brought back what was needed. Before Dr Hurd's arrival, her presence had been welcome in the hospital——as the island doctors' presence had been welcome in her vet's clinic. Two halves of a medical team. . .

Not now. Not with Dr Hurd. . .

Maybe she could again with Niall Mountmarche. He seemed to have accepted her completely as a medical equal. Niall accepted the syringe Jess handed him without comment.

'I want insulin in now and the first litre of saline through within the hour. Then keep right on going—— if we're in time,' he told Sarah. He was swabbing the back of Frank's hand and sliding the catheter into place ready for the IV line, taking the blood sample for elecrolytes in the process.

'The insulin can go in with the first litre. You don't stop the flow until I tell you and I'll tell you when to stop. You're not taking instructions from Dr Hurd for this patient, Nurse, but from me. Move. . .'

'But Dr Hurd. . .'

The nurse stared wildly with frightened eyes. She clearly had no idea who this strange man was——to be marching into her ward and giving orders.

'Dr Mountmarche is a qualified doctor,' Jess said quickly, but the nurse's unease didn't diminish.

'I don't know. . .'

Then her face cleared at the sound of footsteps in the hospital corridor.

'Oh, here comes Dr Hurd now,' she said in relief. 'He'll give me orders.'

'You will do as I say. Now!' Niall snapped. 'There's no time for argument. If you don't then this man will be dead within an hour. Jessie, stay here and see she does what I've asked. Brain her and do it yourself if necessary.' His mouth tightened in a grim line.

'But Dr Hurd won't let me,' the nurse sobbed.

'Leave me to deal with Dr Hurd.'

He hesitated, clearly unsure whether to stop Lionel Hurd in the corridor or stay and risk an altercation in Frank's room. Jess saw his dilemma. A shouting match by his bedside was the last thing that Frank needed.

'We'll be right here,' she said swiftly, and Niall's eyes met hers in a fleeting moment of comprehension.

'You're in charge then, Dr Harvey. OK?'

'OK.'

He nodded, a trace of a smile curving the sides of his mouth. 'Rather medicine than Dr Hurd?'

'Any day.'

The smile deepened. 'So you're sending me to battle. Well, they don't call me the Ogre of Barega for nothing,' he told her, and let his hand drop to touch the back of hers in a fleeting gesture of reassurance.

Then he handed the tray of equipment across to Jessie and walked out of the room.

CHAPTER THREE

JESSIE tried hard not to listen. The voices in the corridor
were muted. One doctor discussing a case with another?

Not likely.

If Frank wasn't so desperately ill she'd have no com-
punction in putting her ear to the door but there was
enough to do in the ward for Jessie's attention to be
fully occupied. She worked swiftly with Sarah to set
up the drip, trying to dispel the nurse's doubts as she
went but aware all the time that the most important
thing was to get the drip going and the fluid and insulin
into Frank's dehydrated body.

Sarah was like a frightened rabbit.

The nurse sobbed as she worked and Jess came close
to strangling her. Finally, as Sarah dropped a bag of
saline, Jess paused.

'Sarah, pull yourself together,' she told her.
'Immediately.'

The nurse gulped on a sob. 'I c-can't. I'm so scared.'

'Why?' Jessie lifted the saline bag and hooked it to
the stand, then fitted it to the needle in the back of
Frank's hand. She gave Frank's arm a reassuring
squeeze as she did so.

'You'll be OK now, Frank,' she said gently, with
more assurance than she was feeling. The elderly
farmer seemed beyond hearing but she could hope. . .
'The insulin's going in. Just try and relax and let it
take over.'

Relax. . .

She looked across at Sarah. Sarah was a
crumpled mess.

'I should have insisted,' Sarah said harshly, self-
blame starting to show through her fear. 'I should have
stood my ground and insisted Dr Hurd come back. I

40

knew something was wrong—but Dr Hurd made me feel like a fool. I should have. . .'

'Trusted your own judgement?' Jessie bit back irritation, trying to imagine how she'd feel coming back to veterinary medicine after a twenty-year absence. She crossed to take the woman's hands and gave them a swift squeeze. It was either that or give in to anger—and anger here would help no one.

'Sarah, you've been a fine nurse in the past and you're a sensible woman,' she said roundly. 'Coming back after an absence of twenty years must make you nervous—but technology hasn't changed so much that you can't tell when a man's sick. You have to trust what your common sense tells you.'

'But Dr Hurd wouldn't come and I didn't think past that,' Sarah gulped. 'I hardly thought about the diabetes. I just knew Frank's leg was infected and maybe the poison had spread.' She took a deep breath.

'Well, maybe it was my own insecurity working there, too. If I was sure of myself I would have thought things through—thought of the diabetes—instead of blindly waiting for orders.' She looked doubtfully down at the bed. 'Oh, Jess, do you think we're in time?'

'I certainly hope so.'

The awful heaving had stopped for the moment. Frank was lying back on the pillows, grey with exhaustion, and Jessie's heart stirred in pity. The fluid was already dripping steadily into his veins—but had they moved fast enough?

She crossed to the bed and lifted Frank's hand.

'I have some good news, Frank,' she gently told the sick man, perching beside him on the bed. She didn't know whether he could hear her but she could at least try. 'We've found Harry. He's tired and hungry but he's asleep in my kitchen right at this minute and as soon as you're well enough for visitors he'll be the first one through the door.'

Lionel Hurd would have a pink fit if he could hear

her make such a promise, Jessie knew. Dogs in Lionel's hospital? Never!

That fight was for tomorrow. Jess would cross that bridge when she came to it.

It had been the right thing to say now, though. The old man's eyes flickered open, bodily ills put aside for an instant. There was relief in the exhausted eyes.

'He's. . . Harry's safe?' he whispered.

'Quite safe,' Jessie promised in a voice that wasn't steady. If only she could say the same for Frank.

'Then I'd best hold on,' Frank managed, and Jess had to lean down to hear his thready whisper. 'For Harry. . .'

'You do that, Frank,' Jess whispered back. 'Please. . . You do that.'

There was nothing more that Jess could do. It was just a matter of waiting now—and hoping that the insulin would stabilise him and the fluids would save Frank's life. And hope that not too much damage had been done. . .

'I'll look after him now,' Sarah whispered, smoothing her apron with grim determination. 'I'm right. Oh, Jess. . . What if Dr Hurd says to take the drip out?'

'He'll do no such thing,' Jessie promised, but she wasn't all that sure. Lionel Hurd had an ego the size of a house. . .and Niall Mountmarche had just marched straight over it.

And Niall didn't appear the sort of man to wave peace flags either.

Jessie walked out into the corridor and carefully closed the door behind her—to find the two men still there.

Lionel Hurd was rigid with anger. His florid complexion was almost beet-red and the hands by his side were clenched into fists. As Jess emerged he wheeled to face her and directed his anger straight at her.

'How dare you, girl?' he snapped. 'How dare you. . .?'

'How dare I what?' Jess asked, her eyes moving past him to Niall.

Niall didn't comment. He stood, a dark, enigmatic stranger. His hands were in the pockets of his riding jodhpurs as he waited.

As if he was waiting with benign interest to see what would happen.

He'd lit a fuse. Now he was waiting for an explosion.

It came.

Lionel Hurd had obviously not been able to berate Niall as he would have liked. Someone claiming to be another doctor. . . One he didn't know. . .

He'd be unsure of his ground.

Jess, though. . . An insignificant girl vet. . .

'How dare you drag someone in to see my patient without my permission?' he remonstrated. 'You have no right. How many times do I have to tell you your place is on the other side of the building, Jessica Harvey, and neither you nor the animals you treat are to step over the boundary? The island board of management will hear of this. I'll have you evicted from this building.'

'It's a privately owned building,' Jess said mildly. 'You can't.'

'Not even with the Health Commission behind me?' Lionel glared at her with something akin to hatred. 'If they hear. . .'

'If they hear anything about Dr Harvey's interference then they'll hear you've treated one of the locals with what amounts to criminal negligence,' Niall interceded. Niall's voice was carefully controlled but Jess had the impression of disgust, well contained.

'I have not. . .'

'You've treated a diabetic suffering from cellulitis with oral antibiotic for over a week with no noticeable improvement and without changing the antibiotic to an intravenous line. One.' Niall touched a finger on one hand. He lifted the next finger.

'Two, as far as I've seen you've done no blood-sugar

tests in the entire time he's been in hospital. No check for ketones in his urine or electrolytes done. Three and four. And he's been vomiting for six hours with you refusing to see him. Five. Nail in the coffin, Dr Hurd. Wouldn't you say? If I were you I'd keep my tail nicely between my legs and not make any complaints to anyone.'

'Who the hell are you?' Lionel blustered. 'Who the hell are you to question my treatment?'

'I'm a qualified medico, believe it or not,' Niall said wearily. 'And I don't want to be involved. Not one bit. You left me with no choice.'

'Qualified. . .?' Lionel stared at him belligerently. 'From where?'

Niall's eyes suddenly narrowed. 'London University,' he said slowly. 'And you?'

'I don't have to tell you. . .'

'And you?' Niall snapped the demand in the tone of someone who was brooking no argument and Lionel's colour rose even further.

'Melbourne,' he spat. 'Not that it makes any difference. Whoever you are, I want you to get the hell out of my hospital. Now. You're not welcome here. Wherever you trained you should know it's unethical to interfere with a patient without their own doctor's consent. So clear off. And take your girlfriend with you.' He cast such a look of sneering dislike at Jessie that she flushed.

'I'm going,' Niall said evenly. He held out a peremptory hand to Jess, signalling her to silence. 'But there's two things you should know, Dr Hurd. One is that I intend to take a look at your credentials. A long look. The second is that if Frank Reid dies then I'll personally make every effort to have you struck off every medical registry in the known world. And I'll take personal pleasure doing it.

'So if I were you I wouldn't interfere with the treatment I've instigated. If I were you I'd be very sure my instructions are followed to the letter.'

And Niall turned and walked out of the hospital entrance, pulling Jessie along with him.

They didn't talk until they were outside and even then there was a good two minutes' silence before Niall spoke. He stood in the sun, taking long deep breaths and staring out at the distant sea.

In the end it was Jess who broke the silence.

'I'm sorry,' she said tentatively, 'to drag you into that. . . It wasn't fair.'

'It wasn't,' Niall agreed and the anger that Jess hadn't heard when he'd been talking to Lionel was all there in his voice. 'How on earth did the island board ever employ such an incompetent oaf?'

'I told you,' Jess said, trying to keep her voice light. 'We were desperate.'

'You realise he'll kill someone?'

'Maybe he won't,' Jess said unhappily. 'Maybe this will give him a fright. If it's just laziness. . .'

'I wish I could think this is just laziness,' Niall growled. 'But it should be instinct to order blood sugars on diabetic patients.' He glanced at his watch and swore. 'Jess, I have to go.'

Strangely, there was a note of reluctance in his voice as if he understood the pressures building up on her and really didn't want to leave.

And Jess didn't want him to leave, either. To go across to her half of the building and try to block out what Lionel Hurd was doing to her friend. . .

To just have to hope that the man really was competent. . .

'Paige is waiting,' Niall said roughly. He looked from Jess to the sea beyond and then back again. His gaze almost seemed to be magnetised to the slim young vet.

Something was growing between them. Something intangible that Jess didn't want to explore.

The Ogre of Barega. . .

It would be better if he went right back to being an ogre. Easier for everyone. . .

Safer. . .

'I. . . We'll be right,' Jess said slowly. And then, as a thought struck her, 'My car. . . It's still on the ridge.'

'I'll organise it to be brought back to the hospital.'

'You can do that?'

'I can do that——keys, please?'

Jess flipped the keys from her pocket.

'Niall. . .'

'Yes?'

'Thank you,' she said simply and watched his face.

'I wish I could say it was my pleasure,' Niall told her, and his face changed. He fingered the car keys and didn't meet her eyes. 'I'm starting to think, though. . . I'm starting to think it'd be better if I'd never met you.'

Mid-afternoon. . .

Mid-afternoon of a weekday and Jess was so far behind that she didn't know where to start.

Lunch?

She'd gone past it. She wasn't the least bit hungry.

She'd promised one of the local farmers to drive out and check a mastitis-affected cow. She'd do that as soon as her car was back. There was normally a small animal clinic at four and she needed to check Harry—— and feed one orphaned wallaby and one tiny wombat.

And worry about Frank. . .

And think about Niall Mountmarche. . .

Ogre of Barega.

All those things she somehow fitted into her crazy day but by the time Jess slumped down at her kitchen table that night it was eight o'clock and her stomach was growling in hunger.

OK, OK. . .

Jess opened a can of soup, made some toast and then slumped down again.

And then looked over to where Harry was lying.

The dog had opened his eyes and was looking at her with definite interest.

Or was he looking at her toast?

Smiling, Jessie carried a quarter of a slice of toast over to where Harry lay. She held it to his mouth and the dog lifted it off her palm with a delicate tongue.

Even half-starved, this dog had manners.

'Hey, Harry,' Jessie smiled, her heart warming in delight.

They shared another slice of toast in companionable silence, the big dog's tail moving wearily back and forth in token wag mode. Finally, replete with toast, Harry settled back to sleep.

He'd make it.

Would his master?

Jessie chewed her bottom lip. She wasn't welcome in the hospital. If she went over and Lionel Hurd was there. . .

She'd be thrown out on her ear.

Still. . .

Lionel usually did a fast ward round at six and then went back to his own quarters on the other side of the building. Jess had her own ideas of what he did then, augmented by the number of whisky bottles found in the hospital garbage since Lionel's arrival.

He'd be well into his bottle for the night, she decided. Maybe it was safe.

She couldn't stand not knowing.

It was all she could do not to tiptoe through the hospital corridors to Frank's room. There was an elderly lady with a sprained ankle in the women's ward and there was no sound there—but there was movement in the men's ward.

Jess stopped and listened and then her face cleared as she heard a woman's voice.

Geraldine.

Geraldine was one of the island's two senior nurses. Middle-aged and competent, she'd elected to do night duty when Sarah started working. By the sound of it Geraldine was talking to Frank.

So at least Frank wasn't dead.

Frank Reid was still an extremely sick man but his grey colour had receded a degree or two. He lay motionless against his mound of pillows but his eyes followed Geraldine round the room and they moved to the door and lit up when Jessie entered.

'Jess. . .'

It was an exhausted whisper but it was so much better than last time she'd entered this room that Jess practically burst into tears.

'Hey, Frank. . .' She crossed to the bed and gave him a swift kiss. 'How goes it?'

'I reckon I'll live. Geraldine's bossing me into it.'

'I sure am.' Geraldine gave Jess a worried look. 'Jess, this is awful. I'm feeling dreadful about it. Sarah's told me what's happened. I knew Frank was diabetic but assumed the blood-sugar tests were being done during the day. Sarah wasn't confident of working nights on her own so we organised her to be on day duty when Dr Hurd would be around to support her—but arrangements seem to have gone badly wrong.'

In other words, Geraldine hadn't been able to supervise Sarah and Dr Hurd had been incompetent.

'It's not too bad,' Jess said swiftly, signalling Geraldine with her eyes to change the subject. This conversation couldn't go further without discussing Dr Hurd—and Lionel was still Frank's treating doctor. Jess smiled down at Frank. 'It can't be too bad, can it? Frank looks like he'll live.'

'And Harry, too?' Frank asked eagerly. 'Tell me, girl. . .'

It was a pleasant respite—to sit on the bed and describe Harry's rescue to Frank and Geraldine. At the end they both stared at her, astonished.

'Well, I never!' Geraldine said roundly. 'The Ogre of Barega turning out to be human. A doctor and a father, too.'

'Yes.' Jessie's face clouded at the sudden remembrance of Paige. There was something there that wasn't right. It was the child who seemed to be haunted—not the ogre.

Her eyes flicked up to Frank's drip. The saline bag was almost empty.

'How many litres has Frank had?' she asked.

'Three.' Geraldine frowned. 'I've another bag ready but Dr Hurd hasn't left any orders. Should I put it up?'

'What would you normally do?'

'Ring and ask him.'

'Then ring and ask,' Jessie said steadily. There was no way that Jess could operate as back-up doctor. Unethical in the extreme and totally unworkable. She stood up and smiled a farewell to Frank. 'I expect Dr Hurd will check you before he goes to bed, anyway. I'll pop in tomorrow.'

She'd pop in during Lionel Hurd's clinic times when he was safely out of the way.

The words weren't said but each person in the room knew what Jessie meant.

Geraldine grimaced.

'Only six more months until our proper doctors come back,' she muttered. 'They can't come back fast enough for me.'

'Or me either,' Jess agreed.

Her long day was finally over.

Jess was more than ready for bed. She showered swiftly, checked her invalid animals one last time and headed for her pillows with speed—only to be stopped by a tap on the door.

Now what?

Jess's flat was at the back of the vet clinic and Lionel's flat was at the rear of the hospital, making four rather unequal quarters to the rambling medical complex.

The door being knocked on was internal—so it was someone from the hospital doing the knocking.

Lionel. . .

Jess pulled on a long robe and buttoned it to the neck. Lionel had knocked on her door after whisky before—and was a much friendlier proposition than the daytime Lionel.

She preferred his daytime aggression.

Jess opened the door an inch—and then pulled it wide. Geraldine.

'You weren't in bed yet?' Geraldine asked, her face creased with worry. 'Jess, I hate to disturb you but. . .'

'Is there something wrong with Frank?'

'No.' Geraldine shook her head. 'He's still recovering. I put the next saline bag up, but I had to do it without orders. Dr Hurd hasn't been back—and he doesn't answer his phone.'

Jess frowned. As the island's only doctor, Lionel Hurd carried a mobile phone with him wherever he went. Even if he was on the other side of the island he should still be carrying it.

Jess glanced at her watch. It was still only nine o'clock. She went to bed early because of her broken sleep with animal feeds—but the rest of the island should be still awake.

'Maybe the phone's not functioning.'

'That's just it,' Geraldine fretted. 'I thought I'd test it. I rang the number and then let it ring while I went to the doctor's flat. I can hear it ringing out in his living room.'

'Then he's gone out without taking it,' Jess said grimly. It broke all the rules of Lionel's contract to do so—but the man was angry enough to do anything tonight.

'Maybe he's down at the pub.'

'No.' Geraldine's face grew more troubled. 'Jess, I think there's something really wrong. . .'

'You mean, he's in trouble?'

'No.' The nurse hesitated. 'When I couldn't find him I rang Sarah at home, thinking at least he might have given her specific orders for numbers of saline units.

One of Sarah's boys reckons he saw Dr Hurd board this afternoon's plane out to the mainland. Sarah thought he must be mistaken—but now I can't find him. . .'

Jessie stared.

Today was Wednesday and on three afternoons a week a passenger jet left for Sydney. One of those afternoons was Wednesday.

'He wouldn't just leave.' Jess shook her head in bewilderment. 'Would he?'

Geraldine met her anxious look. 'There's a spare key to his flat on the master set,' she said diffidently. 'You have the master set, Jess.'

'Y-yes.'

Jess didn't want to use it. To use it was to confirm a nightmare.

The nightmare was real.

Geraldine and Jess opened the door of Lionel's flat and were met by chaos. The flat had been turned upside down and it didn't take more than a moment to see that most of the doctor's belongings were missing.

'He's done a bunk,' Geraldine stammered. She turned to Jess, bewilderment written across her face.

'But why?'

Jess closed her eyes. 'Geraldine, your husband's on the island board of management, isn't he?'

'Yes.'

'When Dr Hurd applied for the locum position. . .do you know if anyone verified his qualifications?'

Geraldine stared. 'I guess. . . Maybe not. I mean, we were desperate. The last doctor had to go in such a hurry. But Dr Hurd. . . Well, why would he lie?'

Why indeed?

'Niall Mountmarche will know,' Jess said slowly. 'He was going to check. I don't know whether it was just a threat or if he really meant to find out if Lionel's qualifications were OK—but it seems Niall Mountmarche has lost us our island doctor.'

'If Lionel Hurd ever was one,' Geraldine said shortly. The capable nurse was almost visibly bracing herself for a rocky future. She met Jessie's look with grim determination. 'Where does that leave us, Jess? Without a doctor at all? And for how long?'

'I guess we still have Dr Mountmarche. . .' Jess was thinking aloud but she hardly believed the words as she said them. 'If Niall Mountmarche is really a doctor himself. I suppose we don't even know that. Good grief!'

'Niall Mountmarche saved Frank Reid's life,' Geraldine said solidly. 'He's a better bet than Lionel Hurd ever was. All you have to do, Jess, is persuade him to help us.'

'Oh, yeah. . .' Visions of the Ogre of Barega flooded back and Jessie visibly flinched.

'Well, at least you know him,' Geraldine reasoned. 'I guess if you don't succeed we can send an island deputation. But I think you should try first, Jess.'

'What, now?'

Geraldine smiled. 'Well, maybe give him until morning. I'll keep Frank's saline drip going overnight. It can't hurt, after all, even if I don't have specific orders. His blood sugar's still dropping. Tomorrow, though. . . Well, I'll need a doctor to assess further insulin dosage and antibiotic levels. So, as long as you talk this Dr Mountmarche into starting by lunchtime. . .'

'Geraldine, I get the feeling the man doesn't want anyone going near the place—much less persuading him to come out on a regular basis. If he doesn't want to. . .'

'He must.' Geraldine spread her hands. 'Jess, you either persuade him to come or we'll have to airlift Frank off the island—plus every other emergency that comes to hand. He has to help us. Surely. . .'

Surely.

'Get yourself a good night's sleep first,' Geraldine

advised kindly. 'It's never a good idea to tackle ogres after a sleepless night.'

'Gee, thanks,' Jess said expressively. 'That really helps, Geraldine. I bet I'll sleep like a baby.'

CHAPTER FOUR

SLEEP like a baby!

Jess slept for maybe all of ten minutes and it was a heavy-eyed vet who drove out to the vineyard the next morning.

The sign was still on the gate.

TRESPASSERS WILL BE SHOT.

'Oh, help,' Jess whispered to no one in particular as she stopped to haul open the gate.

Oh, help. . .

Niall Mountmarche was home. There was smoke curling from the chimney in the still morning air and up on the ridge Jess could hear a tractor working among the vines.

It must be Hugo on the tractor. As Jess pulled up by the farmhouse Niall Mountmarche emerged from the back door.

The man was wearing a pair of jeans and nothing else. Tanned and naked to the waist, the sight of the man almost took Jessie's breath away. The sun glinted on his bronzed skin and Jessie's very proper upbringing was at complete odds with how she felt.

Good grief. . .

'Dr Harvey. . .'

As a welcome it could have been better. Niall's voice was like a douche of cold water.

'Dr Mountmarche. . .' If he could be formal then so could she. Jess climbed from her small sedan and faced him.

She'd dressed a little more carefully this morning—in jeans, to match his, and a clean white blouse. She never looked her age, she knew, but at least this morning she didn't have grubby, scratched knees and her blonde-brown hair was neatly brushed and tied back from her face.

'What can I do for you?' Still the absurd formality.

'I. . . We need your help,' Jess started, her words faltering.

If only the man didn't look. . .didn't look. . .well, so darned male! It was enough to make any self-respecting female get in her car and bolt for cover.

Her mother had never warned her of reactions like this.

'My help?' he asked non-committally and waited for more.

'Lionel Hurd has left.'

'Has he?' Niall's voice grew suddenly thoughtful. There was a bench beside the back door. Niall lifted a shirt from a pile of clothing and absently pulled it on. 'Well, well. . .'

'It doesn't surprise you?'

'No.'

'You scared him off.'

'I guess you could say that.' Niall cast a glance inside the house as though checking that there was no one within earshot and then relaxed a little. 'He's not qualified, you know.'

'I don't know.'

'Well, you damned well should. I made a couple of phone calls last night. The man failed fourth-year medicine. He got himself into some alcoholic mess and dropped out. After that. . .well, he attempted to restart at a couple of interstate universities but never got anywhere. He's in trouble with the New South Wales police for impersonating a doctor and for some scam involving fake cancer therapies.

'I intended to ring the island police this morning after talking to you but it seems the threat of exposure was enough to make our Dr Hurd run.'

'I see.'

Jess bit her lip.

Niall hadn't come near her. He was standing by the

back door as if waiting for her to say her piece and go. Fast.

'How's Frank?' he asked.

'He's recovering.' Jess took a deep breath. 'I. . . We need to know insulin dosages and flow rates for the drip. And the antibiotic regime. The nurses need their orders.'

'You'll have to get yourselves a doctor, then.'

Jess shook her head. 'There are none available. That's why we accepted Lionel. It's October. The medical year ends at Christmas and everyone's safely in jobs until then. Even if there was one free it would take a month to advertise and have them respond.'

'Then you have a problem, Dr Harvey,' Niall said brusquely. 'I'm sorry I can't help you.'

'You can.'

'No.'

There was silence. The sound of the tractor was muted in the hills behind them. There were cockatiels in the high gums around the house, chattering in early-morning excitement.

Nothing else.

'Please. . .' Jess said at last. 'Otherwise, Frank has to go to the mainland. We'll have to arrange an emergency airlift. And it wouldn't hurt. . .'

'Wouldn't hurt who?'

'You.'

'You don't know what you're talking about,' Niall said roughly. And then swore as a child's cry came from inside. 'Dr Harvey, you'll have to leave. . .'

And he turned and walked inside.

Jess didn't.

TRESPASSERS WILL BE SHOT.

The sign's harsh warning sounded over in her head but Jess stayed where she was.

She was fighting for Frank.

And maybe she was fighting for something she didn't understand herself.

She closed her eyes, searching for courage, and then walked into the house after him.

The first room was a massive kitchen, bigger than Jessie's. Like Jessie's, it had a vast slow combustion stove.

Niall was kneeling beside it, holding his waif of a daughter close—and his daughter was screaming.

The child was still in her nightclothes. Although held tight in her father's arms she seemed unresponsive to his hold. Her frail body was held rigid and her distraught sobs were laced with terror.

What on earth was happening?

Jess stayed motionless. She should leave—she should—but there was some instinct within telling her to stay.

Her love of wild creatures. . .

It was what had driven her to be a vet in the first place. She couldn't walk past an injured or distressed animal. And this child. . .

This child seemed to be just such a creature. Lost and bereft. . .

'Niall, can I help?' she asked gently. The child's sobs were going right through her and Paige was holding herself frantically rigid in her father's arms. Niall seemed helpless in the face of his daughter's distress.

'What the hell. . .?' Niall swung to face her. 'Get out of here,' he snapped. 'Now!'

'Not before you tell me what's wrong.' Jess bit her lip, aware that she was intruding in the worst possible way—but also powerless to stop. There was something about this child that cut through her defences like a knife.

Niall wasn't reaching his daughter. The child's sobbing was bereft and frightened as if she didn't know where she was or what was happening to her. She was lost. . .

The ugly callipers stuck out from the little cotton nightdress. The child's hair was unbraided, flowing free round her red-blotched face, and her hands were tightly clenched fists. She was beyond responding to her father, her sobbing wild and terrified.

'Let me try,' Jess said, and walked toward them.

'No.' Niall moved his body in an instinctive act of defence. A hawk protecting his young. The child was pulled closer to him—but there was no comfort for her there.

'I'm good with. . .with little ones,' Jess told him. 'Please. . .' Ignoring his gesture of defence she stooped before Paige and held out her hands.

For a long moment Niall glared. His body was rigid with anger and his eyes were black with it—yet there was also a hint of helplessness. Of hopelessness. Of a man at the end of his tether.

'Please,' Jess said again and then, as though he had assented, she lifted the child away from her father and pulled her to her breast.

Jess didn't say anything. Not a word. Instead, she gathered the sobbing child to her body and held her as close as it was possible for woman and child to be. Cradling the child against her, Jess walked over to a big armchair beside the stove. She sank into its depth, the terrified child still held tight.

'Can you warm us some milk?' she asked Niall briefly and then bent over the child.

She ignored Niall.

For ten long minutes she ignored Niall. Jess was conscious of him—totally conscious—of his dark, brooding presence as he heated the milk and watched the pair in the armchair. She had to put his presence away, though. There was only the child.

This was what she did with her wild creatures—her orphans—when she found them.

Their need was basic: warmth and contact with a substitute mother. No threats until they had learned to trust.

Normally, in the first few days after being found, Jess slipped the orphaned creatures into a pouch and carried them against her breast while she went about

her work. This was what she'd have liked to do with
this little one.

Impossible.

All she could do was to hold this tiny, sobbing girl
close and wait.

Like this child, the animals when she first found
them were rigid with terror. It was a matter of getting
their trust.

A matter of time.

She held the tiny body close, the callipered legs
dangling down but the little face held hard against her
breast. Jess crooned softly to herself, a silly nonsense
song that her mother had crooned to her long ago and
which made no more sense now than it had then.

'Hush, baby. . . Hush. . .'

Hush. . .

It took time but finally, finally, the terror receded.
Jess felt the rigidity leave the child's tiny frame and
felt Paige slump against her, exhausted.

'Hush, baby. . . Hush. . .'

Niall didn't speak. He'd left the milk by the side of
the stove, knowing instinctively that the time wasn't
right. Not yet. He moved around the kitchen, tidying,
filling in time, watching Jess and Paige out of the corner
of his eye.

Waiting.

The sobs ceased.

The child was limp in Jessie's arms but her small
hand had come up to clutch the blouse fabric at Jessie's
breast—and clutch it hard.

Like a lifeline.

Jess leaned over and kissed the top of Paige's head.

'I'd like some warm milk,' Jess whispered softly.
'What about you, Paige?'

There was no answer. There was a slight stiffening
of the body and then Paige relaxed again as she grasped
what Jessie had said. No threat there. Jess signalled
Niall with her eyes and a mug of tepid milk was placed
in her hands.

It seemed that Niall was taking a risk.

Trusting his daughter to a vet.

'OK, Paige,' Jess said gently. 'Let's get you wrapped round this.' She held the cup to the child's unprotesting lips and tilted.

And held her breath.

The child's hand left the fabric of Jessie's blouse. She clutched the mug with both hands and drank.

Jess let out a breath she hardly knew she was holding.

'Now,' she said unsteadily as the milk went down. The child's body was almost relaxed, although she was still holding herself close to Jess—as if drawing warmth from her body. 'What on earth is the trouble?'

'Paige has nightmares.' Niall spoke across the room. He was leaning back against the table, his arms folded, watching Jess and his daughter with troubled eyes. 'She wakes. . . She wakes in terror.'

'That's some nightmare.' Jess gave Paige's thin body a squeeze. 'Horrid.'

'H-horrid,' Paige whispered. The child held her empty mug away from her face and Niall moved to take it.

Paige flinched at his movement and shrank back into Jessie's arms.

Phew. . .

Niall had seen the flinch. Jessie saw it in the man's face—the sort of desperate hurt that cut deep.

'How long have these nightmares been happening?' Jess asked. She had a hard job to keep her voice steady.

'I don't know.' Niall shook his head, his eyes still on his little daughter. 'Paige was with her mother until. . .until five months ago. Then her mother. . .had to leave her and I collected Paige and brought her here.'

'Collected her?' Jess asked, startled. At the sound of her raised voice the child's hand came up and clutched Jessie's blouse again. 'From where?'

'From a hospital in Nepal,' Niall said brusquely. 'The hospital contacted me to say Paige had been admitted with polio and her mother. . . Her mother had to leave. . .'

Jessie stared. The implications of what he'd just said were horrible.

'Polio,' she whispered, her hands tightening round the child's waist as though by holding her closer she could protect her from something so awful. 'But. . .but no child gets polio now. . .'

'Not if they've been immunised,' Niall said harshly. 'Paige's mother didn't think it was necessary.'

'And. . .and you?' Surely the man should have taken some responsibility for his little daughter.

'I didn't even know Paige had been born.' Niall lifted a loaf of bread from the dresser and sliced it with force. 'Until I had the phone call from Kathmandu I didn't know of Paige's existence. I've had a daughter for over five years—and I didn't know. Until the phone call. . .'

'To say Paige was ill?'

'To say Paige was ill.' He slashed down at the loaf. 'Toast, Dr Harvey?'

When in doubt, eat.

It was a principle that had served Jess well over the years. Preferably, when in doubt, eat chocolate but in a real crisis even toast would do.

This was crisis country if ever she'd experienced it. Toast, then. . .

'What do you think, Paige?' Jess asked the little girl, forcing herself to look away from Niall's savage face. She managed a smile down into the child's frightened eyes. 'Shall we have toast? Does your daddy make good toast?'

'Yes,' the child whispered and clung tighter.

Jess smiled. 'Thank you, Dr Mountmarche,' she told Niall. 'Your daughter and I would both like toast.'

Somehow, over the weirdly intimate breakfast, the little girl managed to relax. Jess moved to a chair at the table with Paige still clinging to her. Niall spread hot toast thickly with butter and strawberry jam and by the time Paige and Jess had eaten their third slice the child was sitting in the chair beside Jess and her face was less tense. She seemed almost normal.

Almost. . . There was still a hand clutching Jessie's blouse.

'You know who else likes toast?' Jess asked between mouthfuls and watched the child find courage to answer.

'Wh-who?'

'The dog your daddy and I helped yesterday. Harry. I made toast last night and Harry ate the lot.'

'Did he?' Paige's mouth trembled on a smile. 'Is his leg better?'

'Much better,' Jess said roundly. 'Thanks to your daddy. Your daddy's a fine doctor, Paige.'

Paige looked across at her father as if suspending judgement. 'I would like to see the doggie,' she announced.

See for herself.

There was no trust of an adult world here.

'Harry would like to see you, too,' Jess smiled. 'Maybe you could get dressed and your daddy could bring you down to the hospital. There's someone down there who needs your daddy almost as much as Harry did.'

Where on earth had she found the courage to say that?

She was on dangerous ground here.

Should she talk the man into something via the child?

'Dr Harvey. . .' Niall said and his voice was menacing.

'Yes?' Jess met his look.

'You know what I've said. . .'

'Frank needs you, Dr Mountmarche,' Jess said simply. 'And if Paige is happy to spend some time with me. . .'

'Don't you want to stay here, Paige?' Niall was looking at his small daughter as if trying to work out a puzzle that was beyond him. The anger faded. 'Paige. . .?'

'I'd like to see Harry,' Paige repeated. 'Please, Daddy. . .'

There was a long silence.

'This is emotional blackmail,' Niall said at last and his voice was stifled.

'Frank needs a doctor. And I'll use any means I can to find him one.'

'Including hurting my daughter?'

Paige was concentrating on wiping the last of the strawberry jam from her plate with one sticky finger. The words didn't register with the child—but they did register with Jess.

'No,' Jess said at last. 'Not including hurting your daughter. I'd never consciously hurt any person, Dr Mountmarche. I promise you. . .'

'I've heard promises before,' Niall said heavily. He rose and started clearing plates. His face set as if he was coming to a decision that he didn't like. 'Well, Paige, if you want to go visiting your doggie friend maybe you'd better get dressed.'

'You mean you'll both come?' Jess asked, scarcely daring to breathe.

'We'll come,' Niall said heavily, 'but under protest.'

It took Paige almost fifteen minutes to dress. Jess offered to help but was met with a curt rebuff by both father and daughter.

'No,' Paige said, panic in her voice, and Niall shook his head.

'She dresses herself. She won't have it any other way.'

The child limped from the room on her crutches and Niall and Jess were left on their own.

Looking at the child and then turning to each other.

There was that same tension—as if there was almost a physical link. A chain of invisible silken threads, as strong as steel. . .

'I. . .I appreciate this,' Jess said at last.

'You'd better.' Niall turned from her with a perceptible effort and started hurling dishes into the sink with a force at odds with the softness of his tone. Anger, only just reined in. 'If Paige suffers. . .'

'How on earth would she suffer?'

Crash. A ceramic plate hit the sink and smashed neatly into two.

Jess stared down into the sink at the smashed plate and, despite herself, her lips twitched.

'I hope your plate deserved its fate,' she said primly and Niall wheeled to face her.

And caught her laughter.

He couldn't maintain his fury. He stared down at her, working hard at keeping his expression rigid, but despite his anger his lips twitched in the beginnings of a smile. Somewhere in the depths of those black eyes lurked humour.

'You deserve to have your neck wrung, Dr Harvey.'

'So you're taking it out on the china instead of my neck. Very wise.' Jess grinned and picked up a tea towel as the tension finally eased. 'You wash and I'll wipe?'

'Oh, for heaven's sake. . .'

'You fed me toast,' Jess smiled. 'And I always do my share of domestic duty for those who feed me. Except ironing. Any man who expects me to iron his shirts will have to think again.'

'I'll remember,' Niall smiled and suddenly the electric current was zinging back and forth again with a force that almost shook Jess off her feet.

No. . .

She didn't want this.

'So. . .' She took a deep breath, concentrating on wiping her newly washed plate with much more care than it deserved. 'Tell me about Paige.'

'There's not a lot to tell.'

'Is she so uncomplicated?' It was a rebuke and Niall heard it. His hands tightened on the plate he held and he swore.

'No.' Then he sighed. Niall's hands grew still; he looked out of the window across the slopes of vineyards and Jess sensed that Niall Mountmarche was no longer seeing vines.

'Paige's mother and I had an affair just as I finished medical school,' Niall said at last and it was as if he was talking to himself and Jess had ceased to exist. 'It was a typical university love affair. I was a bit keen on marriage but Karen. . . Well, Karen was a free spirit. She was into alternative lifestyles and freedom of spirit even then and found my medicine anathema.

'On our last night we had a fight about holistic medicine versus traditional and she walked out. For a while I worried about her but I was young and, well, there were other women and a medical career to pursue. Karen was part of my dim distant student days. Until. . .'

'Until?'

'Four months ago I had a call from a Buddhist monk in Nepal. Karen had stayed in a monastery there— heaven knows how or why—and when she left Karen abandoned Paige to the monks because the child was too ill to walk. Paige was just five years old. Karen didn't ask the monks' permission—just did a bunk when Paige's illness got frightening. Like your Dr Hurd.'

'Just left her daughter?' Jessie sucked in her breath in horror.

'I told you,' Niall said grimly. 'Karen's a free spirit. I've found out since that Paige has been farmed out with obliging friends all over the world since her birth. Karen looked after her when it suited her image to have a sweet little girl by her side. The only decent thing I can say about Karen is that she has some good-hearted friends.'

'But when Paige became ill. . . Surely. . .'

'Karen dumped her because the responsibility would have scared her stiff. Not her style—to play nursing mother. I honestly don't know how Paige avoided an orphanage before this.' Niall's hands clenched. 'It might have been better for Paige if she'd been institutionalised. At least she would have had Sabine vaccine. . .'

'And not had polio.'

Niall nodded. His eyes were still far away.

'And when she became ill?' Jess prodded.

Niall shrugged. 'She was very ill, very fast. The monks were worried. A child—especially a desperately ill Western child with no relations in the country—is a heavy responsibility. They carried Paige down to the nearest hospital and from there she was transferred to Kathmandu. She was diagnosed as having polio almost immediately.'

'And how did they find you?'

'She had a small suitcase—pathetic really. Just nothing. No forwarding address for Karen. Not even a soft toy or some reminder of the past. Karen wouldn't have been bothered with a child's belongings. There was only the child's passport and on the passport Karen had scrawled my name and the address I used as a student. Under the relationship section she'd stated I was Paige's father.'

'So one of the monks, and I'll bless him forever, took it on himself to find me.'

Jess licked suddenly dry lips. 'And you are. . .you are Paige's father?'

'Oh, I'm her father all right,' Niall said grimly. 'Her birth date fits. Paige is my daughter and I never knew.' His hands clenched again in the soap suds. 'What gets me is that Karen must have known she was pregnant when she left. . .'

Niall stared sightlessly out of the window and his hands stilled. 'I never even knew she was pregnant,' he said bleakly. 'Karen would have thought it was a wonderfully free-spirited thing to do. Bearing a baby on her own. The only trouble is that Karen would have been trying so hard to appear hip and cool and free that the responsibilities of a child would have come last.'

'And Paige hasn't seen her mother since Nepal?' Jess asked softly.

'Karen won't come back.' Niall's voice was definite. 'She rang the hospital once—once!—and asked how Paige was. They told her Paige's legs were affected and Karen couldn't get off the phone fast enough. ''You'll know what to do,'' she told the interpreter and hung up. I can't imagine Karen facing a polio-affected daughter—and acknowledging it's her fault for not having Paige vaccinated.'

'So. . . So where did that leave you—and Paige?' Jess asked.

'In a mess.' Niall ran fingers through his thick, black hair and soap suds went through as well. He didn't notice.

'Paige wasn't registered at birth as being my daughter so even getting her back into England was a problem. I eventually underwent DNA testing and proved who I was. That, the monk's testimony of Karen's abandonment and some good friends in high places made her legally my daughter. Proving parentage, though, was just the beginning.'

'I can imagine.'

'No,' Niall said bluntly. 'You can't. You can't imagine how hard it is to try and establish a relationship with a child who's never had a father. Her only permanent adult has been transient, to say the least, and she's now abandoned Paige completely. Paige has had to cope with that, plus the pain of polio and these damned callipers. I was at my wits' end to know what to do—and then my uncle died.'

'Louis?'

'Louis.' Niall's voice softened a little. 'Louis Mountmarche was my father's brother and there was a family rift. My father married an Irish girl—hence my name. When he and Louis fell out my father left the family wine business and settled in London. Wine growing, though, was supposed to be my heritage but the first contact I had with it was a lawyer's letter saying Louis was dead.'

'He must have been fond of you—to leave you the vineyard.'

Niall's eyes grew bleak and distant. 'I doubt he was fond of anything. Except his dog. His will left instructions that I care for the dog.'

'I didn't know that,' Jess said softly. 'And, Niall, the dog was so old—and so distressed—I had to put him down.'

Niall smiled then, a self-mocking smile tinged with pain. 'I suppose so. It was just frustration that made me lash out at you. . .'

'So you brought Paige here to get to know her and to give her a chance to know her father,' Jess said thoughtfully.

'It seemed as good a place as any. She's frightened of people. She's still frightened of me. I thought. . . Well, if there was only she and I and Hugo—for however long it takes. . .'

'Hugo?'

Niall smiled again. 'Taking on vineyards full time is hardly ideal with a convalescent daughter. Hugo is my father's cousin. He's always taken an interest in me—and he knows wine backwards. This place has a worldwide reputation—so we decided he'd keep it running.'

'And the awful signs on the boundary. . .'

'TRESPASSERS WILL BE SHOT?' Niall shrugged. 'They were already there and seemed as good a way as any of keeping to ourselves. Until Paige accepts me.'

'But it's not working, is it, Dr Mountmarche?' Jess said slowly. 'Your plan.'

'No.'

Short. Blunt. Savage with pain.

'Why not?'

'She has these damned nightmares,' Niall said harshly. 'There's nothing I can do to stop them and when she wakes she shakes and sobs, sometimes for hours on end. I've tried everything—including sedation.' He shrugged. 'What you saw is her fastest recovery time yet—and it wasn't with me. It was with you. A stranger.'

Jess nodded. 'Her illness,' she said slowly. 'She is convalescing?'

'Yes. She still has major residual weakness in her legs but we're working on that.'

'We?'

'Paige and I.'

'Is that uncomfortable?' Jess asked slowly. 'Physiotherapy to keep twisted limbs straight? I've always thought. . .'

'It's a long and painful process. You're right.' Niall frowned. 'I'm capable of the physiotherapy needed—but she hates it.'

'You know,' Jess said slowly, 'when I'm treating a really frightened animal—one I think stress levels could kill—and it needs an injection or a dressing removed I always try either to have someone else do it or do it in such a way that it can't see me.'

Niall frowned. 'You're saying that if I hurt Paige she won't trust me?'

'She's only a little girl,' Jess told him. 'Not so very different from a wounded joey or fawn. . .'

Niall stared at her. 'Dr Harvey, you're a vet, for heaven's sake. Not a psychologist.'

'OK.' Jess spread her hands. 'I'm willing to be argued down. By a child psychologist. Are you any more qualified than me, Dr Mountmarche?'

'No. But. . .'

'You're a doctor,' Jessie said politely. 'So what special qualifications does that give you?'

'None. But. . .'

'Then pull holes in my argument,' Jess said evenly. 'If I were you, Niall Mountmarche, I would be sitting with that child and cuddling her and cuddling her and not doing a lot else. And if the physiotherapy and general rehabilitation is desperately important then I suggest you get someone else to do it. Bring her down to the hospital. Geraldine's done a massage course and she'd love Paige to bits.'

Niall's face flooded with anger. 'You're saying this to get your own way, Dr Harvey. To get me down to the hospital.'

'I'm saying this because it makes sense.'

'Look, I can't work at the hospital.'

'Are you registered for Australian work?'

'I am—not that your board seems to worry about minor details such as registration and training,' Niall snapped. 'But I'm damned if I'll leave Paige.'

'I agree you can't leave Paige. There's an apartment free, though, Dr Mountmarche. If you need to do night work then you and Paige could stay overnight. While you're doing clinics or house calls we can take care of her. You can let us see how we can help—while you help us.'

'*We...*'

'We,' Jess said firmly. 'Geraldine is a first-class masseuse—and I can help with this little one, Dr Mountmarche. I know I can.'

The trembling that she'd felt in Paige had been the same trembling she'd known in all of her wounded wild creatures. Instinctively Jess knew the path to go— and she knew that she could help both father and daughter.

Without getting involved?

Never get involved with your patients, they'd told her at veterinary school. Once your heart is involved with a patient your clinical efficiency goes out the window. You end up making stupid decisions that aren't in the animal's or the owner's best interests.

It was the one training edict Jess had never been able to follow. Somehow Jessie's heart seemed to get tangled up in every one of her cases.

And how to apply heartlessness to a five-year-old child?

Impossible.

Or was it?

Jess looked up into Niall's drawn, strained face and knew that she was going to have to work desperately hard at keeping her heart uninvolved.

Impossibly hard.

'You mean I should uproot Paige all over again?' Niall asked slowly. 'Is that what you're suggesting?'

'No.' Jess spread her hands. 'This is your home and Paige thinks of it as her home. But you could also have a base at the hospital. Sleep down there when you need to—with Paige nearby and myself and the nurses caring for her. And come here when you can. The medical work's not arduous yet.'

'Yet?'

'There's a hotel being built on the bay,' Jess told him. 'You may have noticed. And plans for more. By next autumn the population of the island looks like doubling with the influx of tourists. But by then our permanent doctors will be back, ready to take over. We only need you until then.'

'And then what?' Niall asked harshly.

Jess stared. 'I don't know,' she said blankly. 'You go back to doing whatever you were doing before, I suppose. I mean, you never intended to stay here forever, did you? Don't you intend to go back to your London medical practice?'

'I suppose I do.'

'Well, then. . .' Keep it clinically calm, Jess thought briskly. 'Will you help us?'

'I don't want to hurt Paige.'

'Then ask Paige if she'll come.' Jessie's eyes softened. She took a step forward and laid a hand on Niall's bare arm. 'We can advertise for a doctor immediately but until then we're desperate. And, Niall, maybe isolating the child here won't force her to trust you. Maybe this is so different to what she's been used to that she can't learn to trust. Maybe. . . Maybe having people around and things going on, with you as the absolute constant, is the way to go. It sounds right to me.'

Niall didn't move. He stared down at Jessie's slim hand on his bare arm and his lips moved into a sneer.

'It sounds convenient to you.'

'That, too,' Jess admitted. She lifted her hand away with an effort. A stupid gesture. . .'But I won't hurt Paige. If I thought. . .'

She stopped as the sound of crutches in the passage signalled Paige's entry. The child hobbled in.

'Are we ready to go, Daddy?' Paige asked and the child was smiling. 'To see Harry?'

Niall looked from Jess to Paige and back again—and then swore softly to himself.

'You'll advertise for a locum immediately?'

'If you won't do it for the full six months. . .'

'I'll do it while you're desperate, Dr Harvey,' Niall snapped. 'I don't like being manipulated.'

Jess shook her head. 'I'm not trying to manipulate you. I'm just. . .'

'Saying it's me or air-ambulancing emergencies to the mainland. If that's not manipulation I don't know what is.' He sighed. 'OK, Paige,' he said and his tone was of a man driven against the wall. 'I'll just have a few words with Hugo and put some things in a suitcase to leave at the hospital in case of emergencies—and then we'll go.'

'Daddy. . .' The child stood stock still. 'Are we going to stay with Jess?'

'Do you want that?' Niall was watching his daughter with eyes that betrayed nothing of how he was feeling.

'Yes,' Paige said definitely. Her small mouth set in a determined line as though here at last was what she was looking for. 'Yes, please.'

And Niall Mountmarche looked like thunder.

CHAPTER FIVE

Jess left Niall and Paige organising themselves and drove slowly back to the hospital. It was still early. She stopped midway and did some overdue herd testing but she was still well on schedule for her morning's work as she turned into the hospital car park.

In the space marked 'Medical Superintendent' was a gleaming black Range Rover.

Niall hadn't wasted time.

Swiftly Jess showered and changed her cow-soiled clothing, checked her menagerie and walked through to the hospital.

Geraldine met her as she walked through to the sister's station.

'You're a magician, Jess,' Geraldine beamed. 'However did you talk the man into it?'

'I'm not sure,' Jess confessed. 'Has he been here long?'

'An hour. He's seen Frank and given me orders and seen old Mrs Fryor, too. Guess what? He says she can go home. He says she's risking making herself really ill lying on her back recuperating from a sprained ankle and he's ordered a walking frame, a few lessons to make sure she's stable and then an ambulance trip home. She's tickled pink.'

'I'll bet.' Jess hesitated. 'Geraldine, have you or have you not been on duty for over twelve hours?'

'Sixteen,' Geraldine grimaced. 'But I thought. . . Well, Sarah doesn't like being on her own and there's the little one. . .'

'Little one?'

'Paige.' Geraldine's face softened. 'Oh, Jess, isn't she a poppet? Her dad's been explaining about her legs. He's going to take Dr Hurd's clinic at one—there are

73

seven patients booked and he's going through their
records now—and I'll massage Paige's legs then and
look after her till he's finished.'

'No.' Jess shook her head. Running Geraldine into
the ground wasn't in her master plan at all. 'You're off
duty. Do Paige's legs now if it's OK with Paige and
her dad and then I'll take charge of Paige while Dr
Mountmarche does the clinic.'

'But you've your vet clinic as well. . .'

'Small animal clinic,' Jess smiled. 'I wouldn't be a
bit surprised if Paige loves it.'

Paige did.

The child endured Geraldine's gentle massage with
stoic indifference to the pain. 'It's enough to make you
cry to see her,' Geraldine whispered as the nurse finally
took herself off duty. 'Now, you're sure you'll be right
with her?'

'I'm sure.'

Jess had to reiterate her assurances to Niall. He'd
done what Jess suggested and stayed out of the way
while Geraldine massaged Paige's legs, and then
returned to comfort his small daughter and take her to
the kitchen for lunch. Surrounded by welcoming
kitchen staff, Paige ate more than she'd eaten for
a week.

'I don't believe it,' Niall told Jess as lunch drew to
a close. 'At the vineyard it's a battle to get her to eat
anything.'

'Maybe this is what she's used to,' Jess said thoughtfully. 'If her mother's taken her from one group of
friends to another—one commune to another, or whatever—then noise and laughter and general chaos won't
be strange. A formal meal with just one or two
people—and both of them male—will be something
she's not used to.'

'Maybe. . .' Niall looked at Jess strangely as if he
was trying to figure out whether she was being imperti-
nent, pushy or just plain sensible. In the end, his

expression said, he hadn't decided. And he didn't much like the sensation.

'I don't like leaving her again this afternoon,' he told Jess bitterly. 'This is some mess you've got me into, Dr Harvey.'

'Mess?' Jess watched Paige drain the last of a huge glass of milk and smiled reassuringly across the table at the child. 'What sort of mess?'

'I mean the medical treatment in this island has been a shambles from the time this so-called Dr Hurd arrived. Nothing's been done. Regular tests have been missed. Every patient booked this afternoon shows some sign of mismanagement on their record. I suppose I have to be grateful that he has at least documented his pseudo-treatments.

'The worst. . . Well, it seems your Dr Hurd has been giving pethidine injections almost on demand. There are three people booked in for what's written up as a regular injection. That alone is just about grounds for having the man struck off—if he was ever on any medical register in the first place. It looks like I'll have to instigate withdrawal treatment for people who never should have been allowed to become addicted.'

Jess flinched. 'I'm. . .I'm sorry.' She shook her head. 'I didn't realise how bad. . . Well, Lionel never let me know what he was doing. I wasn't welcome. . .'

'To stick your nose into his affairs.' Niall gave a bitter smile. 'You seem content enough to stick the same appendage into mine.'

It was a rebuke and Jess's eyes flew up to his. There was a softness there, though, that said that maybe judgement was being suspended. A faint easing of the bitterness. . .

His daughter was at least eating. . .and smiling. . .

'There's a mess to sort out this afternoon if I'm to do any good,' Niall told her. 'Are you sure you have time for Paige?'

For answer, Jess smiled across at the little girl.

'Paige, this afternoon I have to see a cocker spaniel

who was hit by a car last week. I put twelve stitches in his rump ten days ago. Would you like to come and see Harry and then help me take the cocker spaniel's stitches out?'

The empty glass was put down with a thump. Paige grabbed her crutches.

'I'm ready,' she said.

It was after seven by the time Niall finished and Jess was starting to feel incredibly guilty.

She and Paige had worked their way through the ills of the island's small animals and Paige had helped to feed Jessie's orphaned wallaby and wombat. Afterwards Jess had made Paige an omelette. As Paige had finished her tea Harry had stirred in his cage by the fire and decided to show some interest in proceedings. To Paige's wide-eyed astonishment, Jess had made another omelette.

'I thought dogs were supposed to eat dog food.'

'They are,' Jess had smiled. 'But Harry's special. Just like Paige.' She'd eyed the dog thoughtfully as he'd wolfed the omelette and headed for his water bowl. 'Though I think we might take out his intravenous line. That's the tube running into his leg, Paige. When Harry was too weak to eat or drink that's how he got his fluids—but it's starting to seem a bit unnecessary.'

Finally, as Harry had settled down again before the fire and the little girl's eyes had drooped after such a big day Jess had pulled her onto her lap and told her stories until her eyes had closed completely.

There they'd stayed. Paige was as relaxed as Jess had seen her. She'd loved the animals and in her concern for their plight had put aside her own.

As she'd drifted into sleep Paige had put her hand up again to the V of Jessie's blouse and clutched.

'Nice,' she'd said.

Niall arrived soon after.

Sarah must have directed him to Jessie's flat. He knocked once and entered, his eyes lighting up at the sight of his sleeping daughter.

'I thought she might be fretting. . .'

Jess didn't stir. She sat by the fire, Harry at her feet, her arms holding Paige close and her face in the child's hair. She felt strange—as if she had somehow found her rightful place.

Silly. To feel like this about someone else's child. . .

She looked up at Niall and that weird current flashed like lightning from one to the other. It was almost a physical jolt. . .

'I'll. . .I'll put Paige down.' Jess had to fight to get the words out, forcing herself to look away from those eyes. She stood and carried the sleeping child over to the day bed in the corner of the room. Paige seemed dead to the world. There was no chance of waking her.

'How's Harry?'

Niall seemed to be suffering the same trouble. His voice sounded stiff and unsure. The dog stirred and opened one eye in token investigation. Niall walked over, stooped and started gently scratching one ear.

The dog almost purred.

'He's fine.'

'He seems it.' It was as if Niall was searching for something to say. Something to break the link. . . 'This kitchen's huge,' was all he could manage.

'The house was a mansion with this kitchen as the hub.' Jess bent over the sleeping child, her back to Niall, gently adjusting pillows and covering her with a rug. 'When we divided it the hospital cook wanted electric ranges and stainless-steel cook-tops but I loved this kitchen. So we decided this kitchen would be part of my flat and we'd build a new kitchen for the hospital.'

'We?'

'My cousin's the permanent island doctor. He's on the mainland doing obstetrics while his wife finishes her training as a physician. Quinn and I planned this centre.'

'I see.' There was still that physical current and it took a huge effort for Jess to turn round and face him.

'There's a massive amount of money gone into this.'

'Yes.' Jess shrugged. 'Quinn and I put our savings into it—and the island board helped out. On the mainland if you ask for a donation you're looked at as if you're asking for money for someone else. Here if you ask for money the islanders know they benefit and if they can possibly afford it then they'll give. The generosity has been amazing.'

'And you intend to stay here?'

'Yes.'

Unconsciously, Jessie's chin tilted as she turned to face him, as though she was defending her position. Niall smiled.

'I'm not about to evict you, Dr Harvey,' he said mildly. 'I'm just trying to figure out why a young and attractive veterinary surgeon would want to bury herself in a place like this.'

'This place is paradise,' Jess said simply. 'You don't bury yourself in paradise.'

'But your friends...your colleagues...' He frowned. 'You must be one of the most isolated vets in Australia. What does that do to your love life, Dr Harvey? Local farmers? I haven't seen any worthy suitors banging on the door.'

'I don't have a love life,' Jess said flatly and then flushed. There'd been no need to say that. She should have shut up.

'Why ever not?'

Jess shrugged. 'That's none of your business, Dr Mountmarche.' She looked down at the sleeping Paige. 'I... Your daughter and I have eaten. Would you like me to make you an omelette?'

'I certainly would.' There was no hesitation and Niall met Jessie's startled look and smiled. 'Cook tells me hospital tea is at five-thirty so I've missed it by an hour and a half. I told Hugo to expect us if he saw us—and he eats early, too. So it's your omelette or fend for myself—and I make mean toast but not a lot else.'

'Fine.' Jess managed to smile back. 'Take a seat.'

She moved round the kitchen swiftly, trying not to be flustered by his presence. Heavens, she'd fed enough people in her time. She shouldn't be shaken by one dark-eyed, solitary male.

If he wasn't solitary she wouldn't be shaken.

He didn't speak, seemingly content to sit and watch, and Jess gained the impression of weariness only just contained.

For the first time she felt a stab of guilt at persuading him to take this job.

'I've organised the island board to place advertisements in every major Australian medical publication for a new locum,' she told him as the omelette sizzled on the stove. She sprinkled its surface with fresh herbs and flipped it over. 'With luck, we'll find someone fast and you can go back to being a viniculturist—or whatever you call yourself.'

'Wine-grower will do—and I'd appreciate that,' he said slowly, his eyes not leaving her.

'When Paige settles, will you go back to London?'

'I'm not sure.'

'You mean you do want to farm permanently?' Jess asked, startled. 'Instead of practise medicine?'

'As I said—I'm not sure.' Jess ladled the omelette onto a warmed plate and placed it in front of him and Niall looked down in appreciation. 'That's some omelette, Dr Harvey. They never taught you that in vet school.'

'I enjoy cooking. Will you drive back to the farm tonight?'

'I don't think so.' Niall looked across at his sleeping daughter. 'If my promised apartment is prepared then I'll carry Paige over and we'll sleep there.'

'Sensible.' Jessie reached into her fridge and produced a chilled green bottle. 'Especially as it means you can have wine with your omelette.' She smiled. 'It's even Barega wine.'

'Our very own Riesling. And you weren't intending to produce it if I was driving.' Niall's eyes glinted with laughter. 'Has anyone ever told you what a managing woman you are, Dr Harvey?'

'I try,' Jess said demurely and laughed back at him. Their laughing eyes met.

And the weird, magnetic force slammed home with such impact that Jess gasped.

Good grief. . .

What was she getting into here?

She poured the wine with shaking fingers and turned away quickly. She had no idea what was happening and she didn't want to know. This man was threatening her safe, cocooned world and she didn't like it one bit.

Maybe they should have airlifted Frank to the mainland.

Maybe it would have been safer.

A movement by her leg caught her eye and Jess knelt down in relief. Wobble, her tiny baby wombat, was struggling free of his pouch.

'You want your dinner, too?' Jess said in a voice that wasn't quite steady.

At least it gave her something to do. She fed her two orphans with their milk formula while Niall ate his omelette, drank his wine and watched her like. . .

Like a benevolent genie. . .

A genie who'd just produced something magical and was amazed with what he'd done.

Jess wasn't at all sure that she liked the impression.

Finally, her babies tucked back in their pouches, she stood up.

'I'll put Harry back into his cage and take you to your apartment,' she faltered. 'The domestic staff have cleaned it out for you and they tell me it's ready.'

'Cook showed me the general layout of the place,' Niall replied. 'I know where to go. Why does Harry have to go back in his cage?'

'Because he's getting better,' Jess smiled. 'And I don't trust him with my babies. Even if he just sticks his nose into their pouches it might shock them.'

'I see. Well, don't put Harry back on our account.'

Niall stood then, large and overpowering, his presence seeming to fill her kitchen as it had never been filled before.

'Thank you for the omelette,' he said softly. 'And for the wine.'

'It was my pleasure. . .'

'As it was your pleasure to look after my little daughter?'

'That, too,' Jess agreed softly. She looked down at the sleeping child and shook her head in bewilderment. 'How could her mother abandon her? How could she?'

'Heaven knows.'

Jess looked up at Niall. He was staring down at his sleeping daughter and his face was a mixture of pride and love. Love for a little daughter that he hadn't known existed until four months ago!

How many men would leave their career and go halfway round the world to claim an ailing child they'd never been told had been conceived? Niall had gone with no proof that the child was his—only a message from a monk in Tibet and a scrawled note in the back of a passport.

And he'd come here. . . Put aside his medicine in London and brought his daughter to Barega. To find a cure for ills that weren't just physical.

What sort of man. . .?

Jess didn't know. All she knew was that his presence frightened her. The very knowledge of what Niall had done scared the life out of Jessie. She'd sworn not to have anything to do with another man—ever—and here was this man undermining all her determination.

Overwhelming her with his compassion. . .

He turned to her, a question in his eyes.

As if he could read her thoughts.

No. . .

Confused, she turned away to open the door—but Niall was there before her. Whatever the current was that was running between them it didn't have just one

direction. It flooded back and forth with the strengt.
of fire.

'Jess?'

He moved like a sleek cat, somehow propelling himself to stand between Jess and the door. Niall placed
strong hands on her shoulders and gazed down into her
confused, brown eyes.

His confusion matched hers.

And his desire. . .

'Jess,' he whispered, his hands pulling her to him.
'Do you feel this thing, too? This thing between us?
Dear heaven. . .'

Jess didn't reply. She couldn't.

She wanted to pull away. Desperately she wanted to
pull away but her body wouldn't obey.

Instead she stood mesmerised, caught by the desire
in his dark, dark eyes.

Caught by the stirrings of want in her own
slight body.

Of need. . .

She didn't need. She didn't!

She didn't need any man. Not after John Talbot.
Once was enough. She'd been stupid once. . .

The thought gave her strength to pull back but Niall's
hands didn't release her. His hold tightened and his
dark eyes searched hers.

'What's wrong, my beautiful Jessie?' he whispered.

My beautiful Jessie. . .

The words slashed like a knife. She'd been called
that before. Before the pain.

'No. . .' It was a frantic whisper.

'I've told you before——' Niall's voice contained a
hint of concern '——I'll not hurt you. I swear. . .'

'I don't want. . .'

'Me?' He shook his head. 'What's between us,
Jess. . . I don't understand it any more than you do but
I'm starting to think it's something we should explore.
And how else to explore. . .'

His voice fell away. The dark eyes looked straight

into hers, passion flaring in their depths, and he bent his head and kissed her.

Jessie had been kissed before—but never like this.

For a moment she held herself rigid, her body reacting with blind, unreasoning panic.

And then the kiss caught—and held.

It was like the meeting of two halves in a whole. The coming together of parts that had been torn asunder and their rightful place was together.

Niall's mouth caught and held hers and his arms went round to draw her rigid body to his.

She was powerless—powerless to resist the magnet.

Jess had never felt a kiss so full of longing.

There was desire surging through Niall's body—she could feel it—and Jess felt a rush of matching need in hers. Her lips were under his and he kissed her mouth with infinite tenderness—as if he had never touched anything so precious.

How could she hold out against such tenderness? How could she? Especially when every nerve in her body was screaming to respond.

She felt her lips open; she felt her mouth welcome his, tasting his arrant maleness and feeling his need. Her arms went around his hard male body and she clung as if drowning.

It was as if there were two Jessies: one being kissed and responding with all her heart and another standing above her body, staring with horror at this man making love—wanting her—demanding a response with every fibre of his being.

And the first Jessie was winning hands down.

The first Jessie wanted this man with all her heart.

What would have happened next the second Jess— the one above the responding Jessie's head screaming grim warnings—was horrified to think but a gentle tap on the door and then another, more urgent, knock almost brought the first Jess to her senses.

Almost.

It was Niall who drew away first. He stood holding

the dazed young vet at arm's length and the desire was
still there, blazing.

'Damn,' he said unsteadily as the knocking continued and Jess managed a shaky laugh.

'Just. . .just as well.'

'Maybe.' Niall touched her face with the finger of
one hand. 'Duty calls,' he said softly. 'Damn. . .'

He swore and kissed her lightly once again before
moving to open the door.

It was Sarah.

Of course.

The nurse stood staring from Jess to Niall and back
again, clearly confused but too worried to see what was
really happening.

If it had been Geraldine then Jess would have been
in big trouble. Geraldine would have guessed what
she'd interrupted as soon as she'd opened the door.
Jessie's face was suffused with colour. Her breath was
coming too fast for comfort. Something deep inside
was threatening to burst.

Sarah was too concerned with her own worries,
though, to think about what was happening between
doctor and vet. Geraldine's normal nursing partner was
returning from holidays in the morning and it couldn't
be too soon for Sarah. She could go back to helping
out when things were busy—when there was work to
do but little responsibility.

'I'm sorry to disturb you, Dr Mountmarche, but Mr
Reid's drip has packed up,' she faltered. 'I tried your
flat, Doctor, but you weren't there.'

'Because I was here.' Niall grinned, the strain that
seemed almost permanently round his eyes lifting and
lightening. 'Well hunted. I guess you want me to fix it.'

'Y-yes, please.'

'I'll come now,' he promised. He cast a thoughtful
glance at Jess, his eyes glinting at the colour on her
cheeks. 'But I'll carry Paige back to my flat first and
you can stay with her while I do the drip, Sister.'

'I'll do that.' Sarah relaxed. Caring for a child while

Dr Mountmarche took over acute medical care suited her down to the ground.

It was on the tip of Jessie's tongue to say, Leave Paige here. I'll look after her.

She didn't make the offer. The tip of her tongue wasn't working properly. The sensations running through Jessie's body were almost overwhelming.

All she wanted to do was to hide. To be alone. To think through events that threatened to overwhelm her.

She stood aside as Niall gathered his precious bundle, wrapping his daughter in blankets and carrying her to the door.

'I'll bring back the blankets later,' he told Jess.

'No.'

Jess shook her head, refusing to meet his eyes.

'I'll be asleep later,' she managed. 'Morning will be fine.'

'I see.' Burdened with the child, Niall couldn't force her to look at him. His voice was troubled, though. 'Are you OK, Jess?'

'Fine.'

She wasn't fine at all. She was scared stiff.

'I have a clinic booked in the morning. . .'

'Paige can come with me while you work,' Jess told him. 'She's always welcome and there's little I do where she can't watch.' She took a deep breath, still not meeting his eyes, but her voice was almost back to normal. 'My patients don't worry about modesty or confidentiality.'

'I suppose they don't.' It was an absurdly formal conversation.

She wished he'd go. She just wished he'd go.

'Jess?'

'Yes?' Jess was acutely aware of Sarah watching from outside the door. For heaven's sake, the nurse must know there was something going on between them. The tension was almost visible it was so strong.

'I wish you sweet dreams,' Niall said softly.

Jessie's eyes flashed up to meet his—and then

wished she hadn't. His look was a caress all by itself.

'I hope. . .I hope your daughter has sweet dreams,' she managed to whisper in reply. 'That's all I care.about.'

CHAPTER SIX

JESS fed her babies at five a.m. and then set her alarm for seven. It didn't have a chance to go off. Fifteen minutes before it was due there was a series of loud thumps on the door from hospital to flat and then the sound of crutches across the kitchen floor.

'Can I come in?'

Jess surfaced reluctantly from troubled sleep. There was a small face peering round her bedroom door. 'Paige?'

The child was still in her nightdress. She clumped across to the bed and stared down at Jessie's nose emerging from the quilt.

'I knew you'd be awake,' she said triumphantly. 'Daddy said, "Go away it's not even morning," but I told him everyone would be awake. So then he said I could go and find out whether everybody really was awake all by myself and I did.'

'Everybody meaning me?'

'Especially you.' Paige beamed as though signalling a very special honour.

'Your daddy is a very generous person,' Jess said drily.

'I didn't have a nightmare.' Paige laid her crutches on the floor and put both hands on the bed to support herself. 'It's cold out here,' she said hopefully.

'Well, you'd better come in.' Jess pushed back her quilt invitingly and the child scrambled up. In seconds she was cocooned against Jessie's body, her cold toes on Jessie's legs.

'Ooh, you're warm.'

'That's more than I can say for you, twerp,' Jess smiled and obligingly put her arms round the child and cuddled.

It seemed that human contact was all Paige wanted. To be cuddled. To draw maximum warmth from this strange, fearful adult world.

'Daddy's very pleased I didn't have a nightmare,' the child announced. 'Are you?'

'Very pleased.'

'He says we might stay here again. Lots of times. That means I can visit you every morning.'

'Wow!'

'You'll like that?' The child was suddenly anxious, sensing the laughter in Jessie's 'Wow', and Jess gave her thin body a squeeze.

'It'll be delicious,' she agreed. 'Much better than an alarm clock.'

'It sort of seems better here than at the farm,' Paige confided. 'When I'm here. . .I play a game. . .'

Her voice was suddenly shy, as if about to confess something she wasn't sure about.

'What sort of game?'

'That I have a mummy.'

Jess closed her eyes. Instinctively she pulled the child closer. 'Paige, you don't have to pretend,' she said softly. 'You do have a mummy. Your mummy's travelling at the moment but she left you with some lovely people who found your daddy for you.'

'You're talking about Karen,' Paige said scornfully. 'She's not my mummy.'

'Paige, she is. . .'

'No.' The child's voice hardened as if she was reciting a well-learned lesson—one she didn't like a bit. 'Karen says I'm not to call her Mummy. She says only bourgeois children have mummies and I have to learn to be ind-independent and stand on my own two feet. She says the sooner I learn not to need her all the time the better it'll be for me and for her but I sort of think. . .'

The child's voice was a strange mixture of adult and confused child and Jessie's heart melted. 'You sort of think what?'

Paige sighed and snuggled close. 'Well, it's really, really nice to at least have Daddy. But Mummy sounds even better.'

'Lots of kids only have either a mum or a dad,' Jess said evenly, biting back anger at the unknown Karen. 'And Karen is still your mum, even though she wants you to call her Karen. It doesn't make her any less your mum. So you have a caring daddy and a travelling mummy. Exciting, really.'

'I don't think it's very exciting,' Paige said bleakly. Then she pulled away from Jessie's hold and sat bolt upright in the bed. 'Jessie, I can hear Harry. Harry's awake.'

So could Jess. The big dog was whimpering against the door of his cage. Their talk had disturbed him but he was making it known that he was uncomfortable, to say the least. The whimper rose to a whine.

'What's wrong?' Paige almost tumbled out of bed in her haste to reach him. 'Is he hurting?'

He wasn't hurting. Jess reached the cage door just behind Paige's speedy crutches and nodded as she inspected the cage.

'I see,' she said slowly, smiling down at the Border collie. 'Ever the gentleman, aren't you, Harry?'

'What's wrong?' Paige demanded.

'Well, Harry is a very well-trained dog,' Jess smiled. 'For the last two days I've had newspaper in the base of the cage for when he needs to go to the toilet—and he's been too sick to go anywhere else. Now, though, he's starting to feel well enough to remember it's not at all proper to go to the toilet in someone's kitchen. See the newspaper? It's not soiled at all and it's eight hours since I changed it.'

'What will we do?' Paige asked anxiously. The dog was trying to paw the cage with his uninjured leg and whimpering when his weight went onto the injured pad.

Jess had pulled on her warm dressing gown. She slipped back into the bedroom and returned with a thick fleecy jacket.

'Let's put this on you,' she told Paige. 'You've slippers for those feet? Good. OK. I'm going to carry Harry out to the back lawn. Want to come?'

'I sure do,' Paige said triumphantly. 'I knew everyone except Daddy was awake.'

Daddy. . .

Niall Mountmarche. . .

For about ten whole minutes the image had faded but now the remembrance of last night flooded through Jess with a rush of fierce sensation.

How could she have let him make love to her?

The man was so close. A corridor away, sleeping while she entertained his small daughter.

Maybe she'd better put half a dozen advertisements for locums in each medical journal, Jess thought grimly. How on earth could she face the man now?

Jess carried Harry gently out to the back lawn of the hospital, where the headland ran right out to the sea beyond. It was a magic spring morning, the sun already holding a promise of warmth, and there wasn't a breath of wind. The only sound was the surf from the distant sea.

Jess set the dog down on the grass and Harry did what he had to do with an almost audible groan of relief. Then they watched while Harry proceeded to sniff his way round unknown territory.

He hopped on three legs, carrying his injured pad high, Jess was pleased to see, and not attempting to bear weight on it yet. The bandaged pad seemed almost a trophy. Harry's bright eyes cleared and he looked around with the air of a dog almost content with his lot.

Almost.

There was a hint of unease.

Jess had saved his life but Jess wasn't his master.

'He looks like he wants something,' Paige said, and Jess nodded.

'He wants someone.'

'Like his mummy?'

'Like his dad.' The voice came from the hospital

door and made Jess jump. All three—child, woman and dog—turned to face the voice. Niall Mountmarche was standing on the top step, surveying them with complacency.

'I thought you'd run away,' he told his little daughter with a smile.

'I wouldn't!' Paige's face was appalled as if she couldn't imagine doing something so stupid. She clutched Jessie's hand as if for support and Jess realised that Paige still wasn't completely relaxed with her father.

Niall was a strange new man in the child's life. Who could blame Paige for her mistrust?

Who could blame Jessie for the same mistrust?

'I only went to Jess,' Paige whispered.

'On her father's recommendation, I understand,' Jess managed. Instinctively she pulled her robe more tightly closed. 'See if the world's awake, did you tell your daughter? And if they're not then wake them up.'

'I like sharing the joys of parenting,' Niall said easily. Unlike Jess, he was showered and dressed—in casual slacks and open-necked shirt. He strolled across the lawn towards them, pausing as he came to welcome Harry's curious advances.

A man content with his lot. At ease with the world.

He smiled at Jess and the force slammed back.

'He's. . . Harry's better. . .' Jess whispered. Dear heaven, why did she react like this?

'I see that.' Niall gave the dog a final pat and straightened. He smiled down at Paige. 'You've been helping Dr Harvey look after him?'

'Dr Harvey's name is Jessie,' Paige said solemnly. 'She doesn't like anything else. Jess is pretty.'

'She is at that,' Niall smiled, and his eyes moved back to Jess. 'And some!'

Jessie flushed bright crimson.

'I. . .I'll leave your daughter with you,' she stammered. 'Harry's been out for long enough. I'll take him back to his bed by the fire.'

'Frank's awake.'

Jessie's eyes flew to his.

'Why don't we take Harry in to see his master?' Niall said easily, smiling down at her flushed face.

'I'm not even dressed,' Jess told him, grabbing the gown and pulling it tighter.

'So I see.' His eyes laughed at her, watching the defensive measure of her hands. 'But you look great to Paige and I—and Frank will have eyes only for his dog.' He turned his attention to Harry who'd sat down at Niall's feet as though waiting. His bandaged paw was still held out in front. 'Does Harry need to be carried?'

'I'll carry him,' Jess said. 'I don't want him overdoing it yet.'

'He needs to borrow your crutches, Paige.' Niall smiled and scooped the big dog up into his arms. 'Border collies are supposed to be the smartest dogs in the world but they've never managed crutches. It just shows how smart little girls are. OK, ladies, let's pay a social visit to Mr Reid.'

He strode into the hospital with his black and white burden and there was nothing for Paige and Jessie to do but follow.

The reunion was all that Jess could have wished.

Frank had slept most of yesterday, like his dog, exhausted by his body's ills. He hadn't asked to see Harry and Jess hadn't offered, unsure of Niall's reaction.

There was no asking now. By the time Jess and Paige reached Frank's ward the dog was a bundle of shivering delight on the bed with Frank and practically licking him to death. There were grassy footprints on the bedcover. Geraldine would have a fit but it was hard to know who was more pleased to see the other— man or dog.

'What do you think of bringing Harry's bedding in here while there's no one else in the ward?' Niall suggested to Jess. He was grinning down at man and dog as if he'd engineered the whole reunion. 'We can open the French windows and Harry can wander in and out at will.'

Jess stared. 'And the Health Commission?'

'Are a long way away, I think you said, Dr Harvey,' Niall smiled. 'And I can think of no better tonic for Frank.'

Jess looked down at the elderly farmer's shrunken frame and her eyes clouded. 'He's still ill. . .' Frank was muttering endearments to his dog and was out of hearing.

'If I could find Lionel Hurd I'd be tempted to kick him further than he's gone,' Niall said grimly. 'The diabetes has run out of control for months—and it'll take a while to settle. I can't judge long-term damage. But. . .' he shrugged '. . .at least now. . .'

'At least we have a competent doctor.' Jess bit her lip. 'I. . . We do appreciate it.'

'I'll bet.' He cast a curious look at her. 'Breakfast, Dr Harvey?'

'Jessie,' Paige corrected and Niall smiled.

'Breakfast, Jessie?' he amended his question but Jess shook her head.

'I haven't showered.'

'Cook says breakfast is at seven.'

'I eat my breakfast alone,' Jessie told him and turned away abruptly. 'Send. . .send Paige down to me when she's ready. I'll be in my flat—or over in the clinic. She'll find me. . .'

'Alone?'

'Yes.'

'Is that the way you want it, Dr Harvey—Jessie?' he asked and his eyes gently mocked her.

'Yes,' she said again and walked quickly out of the room.

Jess didn't see Niall again for the rest of the day—and that was how she wanted it.

It took trouble to organise. The hospital building was too small by far.

Niall's presence filled it. Even if she couldn't see him she could hear him, joking with the nurses, giving orders, moving out into the waiting-room to collect another patient. . .

It was as if he'd been the island doctor for all his life and not just for two days.

Two days. . .

She'd known him one more day than that, Jess thought fearfully. So. . .

So she didn't know him at all. She knew him less than she'd known John Talbot when first she'd gone out with him.

And that had come close to costing Jess her life.

So. . .

So keep yourself away from him, she told herself fiercely. You know what happened last time. This man has a life of his own—a medical career in England and a life I know nothing of. Even his daughter doesn't trust him.

Maybe it wasn't Niall Mountmarche she didn't trust. Maybe it was the reactions of her own wayward body.

Jess sent Paige to the hospital kitchen for lunch but ate alone. She did when she was busy.

She wasn't busy today. She just didn't want to spend any more time with Niall Mountmarche's eyes on her.

Afterwards she expected Paige to return. Instead Jess did the small animal clinic on her own, working through a stream of animal ills until four o'clock.

As she emerged from seeing her last patient—one egg-bound chook—Niall and Paige were seated in her small waiting-room.

'C-can I help you?'

It was a crazy question to ask but Jessie's head wasn't working normally. There were things going on that she didn't understand and didn't like. Not one bit.

'Paige and I are on our way home,' Niall said

gravely. He stood and his eyes were careful—watch-ful—as though he was trying to figure Jessie's reactions out. 'I've finished Friday clinic. There's only Frank in hospital and he's doing fine—so, with luck, we'll have the weekend on the farm.'

'But we'll come back Monday,' Paige said anxiously. 'Daddy promised.'

'That's great.' Jess tried to smile. 'I. . .I'll see you then.'

'Ask her, Daddy,' Paige said anxiously. 'Ask her.'

'My daughter's arranging my social life,' Niall smiled. 'We wondered if you'd like to come to dinner tonight.'

'No.'

The word was out before she could soften it. It was as if Jess had put up both hands in fear.

'Jess, we'll hardly bite!' Niall's words were humor-ous but there was a question behind his eyes.

'I. . .I know. It's just. . .I have my animals to feed.'

'Isn't there someone you can organise to do that?'

'Geraldine's daughter does them sometimes,' Jess admitted, 'but I don't like asking her unless. . .unless it's something important.'

'And dinner with us isn't important?'

Niall's dark eyes were smiling but the question stayed.

'I can't. . . Please don't ask.'

'I see.' He nodded. 'Jess, the first time I met you, you were as scared as Paige. Why, I wonder?'

Jess took a deep breath. 'Who wouldn't be?' she managed lightly. 'All those signs. . . And you were carrying a gun.'

'We'd heard howls coming from the creek.' Niall leaned back against the wall of the surgery and crossed his arms. He looked like a genie playing a game with his favourite toy. 'I thought there might have been an injured animal—so I took a gun down in case I had to put something out of its misery. In fact, Hugo and I had decided it must be an injured fox.'

'There are no foxes on Barega.'

'I know that now. Frank told me.'

'Bully for Frank.' Jess crossed to the door. 'If you'll excuse me. . .'

'You still haven't told us why you're scared.'

'I'm not scared.'

'Then why won't you come to dinner?'

'Because I'm busy,' Jessie snapped. 'I have responsibilities. . .'

'Then tomorrow for lunch?'

'No.'

'Don't you like us, Jessie?' Paige asked sadly and Jess fought to recover calm.

'Of course I like you, Paige,' Jess told her, crouching to meet the child's worried look. 'But you know I can't leave my animals.'

'You do every time you do a house call,' Paige corrected her. 'Why don't you do a house call on us?'

'Because you'll get sick of me,' Jess told her. She straightened. 'Paige, you live on your farm and I live here. I'll see you on Monday when your dad does a clinic. But for the weekend. . .I need to be alone.'

'Why?' Paige asked and Jess shook her head.

'Because,' she said stubbornly and could think of nothing more to add. It was a child's excuse—and that was how she felt. Like a scared child. She held the door for Niall and his daughter to leave. 'I'll look forward to seeing you both on Monday. But not before.'

Niall nodded slowly. 'I think we can take the hint,' he said evenly, scooping his little daughter up into his arms. 'It's just you and me for the weekend, Paige. Can you cope with that?'

'I s'pose so,' Paige said sadly. 'But I love Jess.'

'But Jess doesn't trust us,' Niall told her. 'I guess it's up to us to figure out how to cure that.'

Jessie had two long days without seeing either Niall or his daughter.

Niall visited Frank briefly on Saturday and Sunday

morning, checking his medication and assuring himself that all was well but Jess managed to be safely out of the way both times. The good thing about Niall having a distinctive vehicle was that she could hear it approach and duck for cover.

She was behaving like a frightened schoolgirl, Jess knew, but she couldn't stop herself.

She'd never been so frightened in all her life.

And for the life of her, she didn't know what she was frightened of.

Fern and Quinn telephoned from the mainland on Sunday morning for their regular update on the island's happenings. Dr Fern Rycroft and Dr Quinn Gallagher, husband and wife, were the island's permanent doctors and were due back at the end of summer.

The couple were appalled to know what had happened.

'But tell me about Dr Mountmarche,' Fern demanded as Jess finished outlining the story. 'Is he a permanent resident on the island? Will we have three doctors instead of two?'

'I wouldn't think so,' Jess said shortly. 'The idea is that he cures his daughter and then goes home.'

'Back to England?'

'Back to England.'

'I see.' There was a long silence at the end of the line. Then Fern finally continued, 'Jess, you don't think he could be talked into changing his mind, do you? If we offered him a permanent job?'

'There isn't enough work for three doctors on the island.'

'There might be,' Fern said cautiously. 'Especially. . .especially if one of the doctors is pregnant.'

Another long pause.

'You're kidding,' Jess said blankly.

'Kidding is right.' There was a chuckle on the other end of the line and Quinn came on. 'Kidding is right,

Jess, love. Kid number one, due next April. Congratulate us.'

'That's. . .that's wonderful,' Jess managed.

'This Dr Mountmarche. . . Is he good?'

'It's too early to say. Better than Lionel Hurd, at any rate.'

'Well, thank heaven he's there,' Quinn told her. 'Otherwise one of us would have been forced to come home—and we really need to finish these training stints. Jess, find out about him and if he's OK, talk him into permanence. A part-time medical practice with his winery might suit him and us magnificently. I'll set some enquiries into motion from this end.'

'Quinn, I don't want to.'

Another silence.

'Why not?' Quinn asked cautiously.

'Because. . . Quinn, I hardly know him.'

'Well, get to know him,' Quinn ordered. 'And talk him into staying. If he's good we could have the best staffed island in the South Pacific.'

It was easy for Quinn to say.

He didn't have to work with Niall Mountmarche. . .

The two men might get on, Jess decided as she tried to think things through without emotion.

It was only Jess who might have to leave if Niall Mountmarche stayed.

There had to be some way she could face him without feeling like. . .like her world was blowing round her like dandelion seeds in a high wind.

The weekend was medically peaceful. Almost unnaturally so.

Jess had learned to mistrust the peaceful times. It was almost as if the world paused before a crisis so that it could catch its breath.

The calm came to an end as Sunday afternoon drifted to a peaceful close. The telephone rang in Jessie's flat.

'Jess. . .'

Why did her breath do that? Catch in her throat at the sound of Niall Mountmarche's voice?

'Yes.'

'Problem, Jess,' he said briskly as if he hadn't heard the sharp intake of breath. 'Can you come?'

'Paige?' Jessie's breath was suddenly caught in fear and Niall heard it.

'Paige is fine. It's an animal problem.'

'Oh.'

'I had a call on the mobile phone Geraldine so kindly arranged for me. One of the local fishermen—Ray Benn—do you know him?'

'Mmm.' Ray Benn had a five-acre plot just outside Barega township where his wife and kids kept a menagerie of different animals. At any given time there was always an egg-bound chook or a dog with a grass seed in its ear or a cat with kittens. 'I know the Benns.'

'There was a local gymkhana this afternoon. One of their kids—ten-year-old Sam—was riding Matilda and came off. He's given his knee a fair thump and they were worried it's broken. I'm sure it's not.'

'But. . .'

'I'm out at their place at the moment,' Niall told her, 'and I was thinking it'd be an idea if you were to have a look at the horse.'

'Has Matilda hurt herself?'

Jess had never been asked to treat the horse but she knew her. Matilda was a placid old brown mare, gentle and knowing. An ideal children's horse.

'No.' Niall hesitated as though unsure of his ground. 'Look, there may be nothing wrong but the family's worried and I don't like the look of her. Matilda bucked Sam off and then kicked him while he was down. She seems almost wild—and they all tell me she's never like this. I wondered if it'd be worth you having a look.'

'I'll come.'

Matilda bucking? Jess frowned. There had to be something wrong. Despite the distraction of Niall's voice, her mind started racing. 'Tell the Benns I'll be there in ten minutes.'

'I'll wait,' Niall told her. 'I'm interested.'

'There's no need.'

'No.' She could hear the smile on the other end of the phone and Jess flushed. 'I know there's no need. But we're medical partners, after all, and you might want a hand. I'm staying.'

'I don't need a hand.'

'You've got one whether you like it or not,' he said bluntly. 'I'm staying.'

CHAPTER SEVEN

THEY were all waiting for Jess when she arrived.

She saw them as she rounded the last bend in the road and her nervousness lifted.

What a reception committee!

The road gate was a steel swing-gate and Jess could count eight heads over the gate. Ray Benn. Five assorted little Benns. Paige. And Niall.

Ray and Niall were chewing grass straws—as though Niall was country-bred and not a London doctor, for heaven's sake—and indulging in slow country talk and the kids were avidly waiting for Jess.

The gate was swung open before she arrived and Jess pulled up, laughing.

It was almost enough to let her forget her nervousness—to forget what the sight of Niall Mountmarche did to her.

Almost.

'It must be a heavy gate,' she smiled as the children all pushed the gate closed and Paige emerged from the throng of children to claim Jess as her own.

The child seemed happy in this crowd of strangers— and Jess had to remind herself that this would be what Paige was accustomed to. Strangers were familiar.

It was family that was strange to Paige. The child was learning only slowly what having her own people meant. Having a parent who was prepared to face his responsibilities...

'We're really worried about the horse,' Paige told Jess importantly. 'And I told everyone you'd know what to do.'

Jess ruffled the child's hair in affection, carefully avoiding Niall's eyes in the process, and turned to Ray Benn.

'What's the problem, Ray?'

The fisherman shook his head.

'That's more than I can tell you, Jess,' he said heavily. 'The horse seemed out of sorts this morning when we loaded her in the float. Took me fifteen minutes to get her into the box and normally she comes in like a lamb. I couldn't figure out what was what. If Sam hadn't been so keen to ride—he's been practising for months—I would have given up and left her at home.

'Didn't do us any good, anyway. She was hopeless in the ring. Didn't do a thing Sam wanted and they're normally a great little pair. Then, as they finished the event, danged if Matilda didn't just up and throw Sam off—and then kick out at anyone who came near.' He scratched his head. 'She's never done such a thing before.'

'Has anything happened to her over the last few days? Anything to give her a shock?' A horse sometimes reacted to a fright by being extra-sensitive for a few days afterwards.

'No. Nothing. I tell you, Jess, she's never been like this and we've had her ten years. I thought she must be coming down with something and asked the doc to have a look after he'd fixed Sam's knee.'

Jess did meet Niall's eyes then and a smile flashed between them.

How many times had Jess been confronted with this? Because she was a vet she was expected to know general medicine. So, while she was here, could she just have a look at Tommy's rash or Mary's sore throat—or even, once, Grandpa's piles! It seemed, then, that for doctors it was the same. While you're treating Sam's knee could you just have a quick look at our horse. . .

'And can't Dr Mountmarche diagnose the trouble?' she asked demurely and got a wicked look from Niall for her pains.

'The doc said we ought to ring you,' the fisherman told her. 'I dunno, though, Jess. It was worth asking him. You can claim a doctor's visit on the health fund and you can't claim for a vet.'

Jess stifled a smile and grabbed her bag from the back seat of her car. The Benns weren't a wealthy family. Ray Benn had worked as a fisherman's hand until he was in his thirties and it was only by scraping and saving every cent that he was able to buy his own boat and this little plot of land to raise his family.

'Let's have a look at her, then,' she said and they set off—the whole entourage.

'Feel like the Pied Piper?' Niall laughed into her ear and Jess grinned back.

It was exactly how she did feel.

The laughter died when she saw Matilda.

Ray had put the horse in a small paddock beside the house. The old brown mare stood backed into a corner, ears stiffly upright, nostrils flared and her eyes wide with fright. She looked almost haunted.

Jess took a deep breath.

'Can you take the children inside?' she asked Ray. 'She's obviously nervous—and I prefer to examine her alone.'

A horse like this was unpredictable—even dangerous. She didn't need an audience.

'I dunno. . .' Ray said doubtfully. 'Do you reckon you'll be right on your own?' He looked at the crowd of children. 'The missus is out with the water truck— she says it's easier to cart water than to look after this many kids—or I'd send 'em all in to her and help but. . .'

'I'll assist Dr Harvey,' Niall assured him. One small boy had just been edged off his place on the fence by his big sister and the early signs of World War Three were obvious. The horse was visibly flinching at the noise.

'I can manage. . .' Jess protested—but not too hard. There was something badly wrong here and she wouldn't mind some back-up. Even Niall. . .

'I'll stay,' Niall said firmly. 'If you remember, Dr

Harvey, I was first medico called in. You're just here in a consultant capacity.'

It took time to get near the frightened horse and by the time she did Jess was really worried.

This was no mere fright.

Under firm instructions, Niall stayed where he was.

'She's scared stiff,' Jess told him. 'I don't need anyone. . .'

'And if she kicks?'

'Then I might need someone,' Jess acknowledged with a rueful smile. 'So stay where you are and wait. If you're lucky you might have a case to care for as I go down to a hoof. If I'm lucky you won't.'

'Good luck, then,' he smiled and his heart-stopping smile was a caress. 'You be lucky. I hope I'm not.'

Niall Mountmarche folded his arms in a gesture that Jess was beginning to know, leaned back against the fence and watched.

Jess tried to block out his presence. Tried and failed.

The fact that she found his presence reassuring was almost infuriating.

Concentrate on the horse.

'OK, Matilda. . .' She spoke gently to the mare and watched the nostrils flare. 'OK. . .'

One step at a time. . .

Finally she reached her. Jess gently slipped her hand into the horse's bridle and patted the soft brown head. The horse's fear remained.

What was wrong?

Jess examined her with care, whispering softly as she ran her hand over the brown coat. Once she raised her voice above a whisper and the horse tried to rear away in fright.

It was as if noise hurt. . .

The mare's eyes were strange—different. The third eyelid was visible and the pupils seemed dilated. For a horse to compete in a gymkhana like this. . .

She must be growing worse. Ray would never have

tried to transport her like this—or risk putting his son on her.

Jess moved the horse gently along the fence, her hand tight on the bridle.

'Come on, girl. Gently. . .'

There was a stiffness there—almost arthritic—and a definite tremor to the back legs.

Something. . . There had to be something. . .

She needed help. Jess turned to Niall and signalled him with her eyes.

He wasn't stupid. Niall had seen what happened when Jess raised her voice. Without speaking he climbed the fence with careful unhurried movements and came toward them slowly—as aware as Jess that this was a horse on the edge of panic.

As soon as he was close enough Jess took his hand and guided it to the bridle, indicating again with her eyes that she wanted the horse held.

Niall's strong hand touched hers again as he took the bridle, signalling that he'd understood. He took control of the horse, his spare hand coming up to run down the mare's trembling face.

Jess stood back and looked.

She ran her eyes all over the big brown body, searching for something that she didn't want to find. Then she knelt and looked again.

It was there. Just above the hoof on the left foreleg. . .

A recently scarred wound. Not big. Half an inch long, maybe, but it must have been deep. The scab had almost fallen away. Three, four weeks old?

The timing was right.

Everything was right.

Or everything was wrong, depending on how you looked at it. For a vet wanting a diagnosis things were right. For Matilda things were very badly wrong.

Jess straightened from where she'd been crouching and the horse sidled, fighting against Niall's hold. She took the bridle from Niall.

'We need a warm, dry stable,' she whispered to

Niall. 'One as far from the house as possible. Can you go and tell Ray to organise it and I'll bring the horse after you?'

Niall cast her a doubtful look.

'Problem?'

'Tetanus.'

There was a moment's silence.

Then, very softly, Niall swore. Without another word he went to do her bidding.

'How long since she's been vaccinated, Ray?'

With the horse safely installed in a stable, Jess stood in the house yard with a grey-faced Ray.

'Oh, Geez. . .' The farmer put his hand to his face. 'I dunno. . . We had her done last time she foaled, I reckon, and that was four years back. There was only a visiting vet once a month then—and afterwards, well, it never seemed worth the trouble. I mean, tetanus is rare, isn't it?'

'Not as rare as I'd like.' Jess sighed. She reminded farmers of the need to vaccinate annually but as she'd never been called on to treat Matilda the old horse had missed her attention.

'Is there anything you can do?'

Jess looked at Ray. The fisherman was almost rigid with distress and her heart warmed to him. To hear Ray with the other fishermen on the wharf you'd think he was as rough as bags but he was marshmallow at heart—and he loved the little horse.

'The treatment for tetanus is often not effective—and it's expensive,' she told him, doing rough calculations in her head. Even if she gave the drugs at cost and didn't charge herself. . .

She told him the approximate cost and Niall's face changed.

Ray didn't flinch. 'Look, we have to try.' The big man spread his hands. 'I've had Matilda longer than we've had most of the kids—and to think I brought this on her by not vaccinating. . . The wife'll be beside herself.'

Jess nodded. 'Do you want to talk to your wife about it first?'

'No. Treat her,' he said roughly. He shook his head. 'It's been a dry winter and one of our big tanks sprang a leak. We're having to cart water and Marg's working herself into the ground to keep the garden going. This is all she needs!'

'We're having trouble in the vineyard, too,' Niall said sympathetically, diverting his attention from the horse for a blessed moment. 'If we don't get rain soon. . .'

'We'll be in trouble,' Ray said savagely. 'I told Margy that last night—and here's big trouble thumping down on us, anyway. Do what you have to do, Jess, girl. We'll pay for it somehow.'

There was little enough that Jess could do. She drove back to the clinic and returned with tetanus antitoxins.

On her return she was surprised to find Niall's Range Rover still in the yard. Paige was seated in a pool of kids and dust, playing a noisy game of marbles, and Jess looked down at the laughing little girl and saw why Niall had stayed.

He'd do a lot for this little daughter.

Niall moved with Jess into the stables, holding the mare while Jess injected the medication and carefully padded each of the mare's ears with cotton wool.

'It'll reduce the noise level as much as it can be,' she told Ray as she and Niall emerged from the stable. 'But it's worth telling the kids to be quiet. The less noise there is the lower her stress level.'

'Yeah, well it's school again tomorrow, praise be,' Ray growled. 'That'll keep them quiet.' He hesitated. 'What odds, Jess?'

'Low.' It was no use dissembling. 'I'll come back in the morning.'

'Right.' Ray almost visibly braced his shoulders. 'OK, you kids. I want you all inside watching the telly.

I know I'm usually kicking you outside but Matilda needs quiet.' He looked from Jess to Niall. 'Can I offer you people a cuppa——or a beer?'

'No, thanks.' Niall shook his hand. 'There's a kettle on at the vineyard——and Dr Harvey's promised us a visit. Isn't that right, Dr Harvey?'

'I don't. . .' Jess started but was interrupted by Paige.

'Yes,' the child said definitely. 'Hugo and me made chocolate chip cookies this morning especially in case you came. And now you have to drive practically past our front door to get home. So you'll come.'

It was a statement of satisfied fact and Jess couldn't argue. She didn't have a leg to stand on.

Jess drove slowly to the Mountmarche vineyard, full of misgivings.

Why had she agreed to this?

Afternoon tea with a child and her two male relatives? What could be more harmless than that?

Fine, if one of the male relatives wasn't Niall Mountmarche. . .

She passed Marg Benn on the road. Marg's ancient truck was carting water from the bore at the south end of the island. She waved her hand in cheery greeting to Jess, not knowing what lay in store for her when she returned home.

A dying horse. . .

Could Jess save Matilda?

She didn't like her chances, Jess thought drearily. Matilda was old, and the disease was known to involve months of recovery even in young, fit horses.

Marg was in for a hard time.

'Please. . .' Jess whispered as she gripped the wheel and turned into the Mountmarche vineyard and her plea was for two things in varying degrees of urgency.

Please let Matilda live.

That was the big request.

But there was another, niggling behind.

Please let me not make a fool of myself here and get

out of this time with Niall Mountmarche with my heart
and my pride intact. . .

Niall and Paige beat her home.

Jess emerged from her car to find Paige almost running across the yard toward her, crutches flying.

'Hey, whoa. . .' Jess caught the child in her arms and
lifted her high. 'You're supposed to be careful.'

'Not when you're coming.' Paige looked behind to
where her father was watching with lazy amusement.
'Aren't we pleased to see her, Daddy?'

'Very pleased,' Niall drawled with his lazy smile
and Jess burned crimson.

'I. . .I can't stay long.'

'Daddy said he bet you couldn't,' Paige nodded.
'But come inside and have a cookie. They're really,
really good!'

'They're even edible,' Niall grinned and somehow
Jess found herself smiling.

The tension eased.

It eased even more when they went inside. Hugo
was already settled behind the tea kettle. The elderly
man seemed almost a grandfather figure to Paige and
it was clear that he regarded the child in the same light.
He smiled at Jess and made her welcome but he clucked
over Paige with the anxiety of a mother hen.

'You've been good for Paige, Dr Harvey,' he told
her with just a trace of a French accent. 'She's more
cheerful now than since her dad found her.'

Jess didn't have to answer. She was finding it hard
to concentrate on anything other than Niall's presence
beside her at the table but the conversation flowed over
and around her and she wasn't pressured.

It was as if they were all giving her time to
acclimatise.

Hugo and Niall talked easily about the vines. There
were problems with water here too, it seemed, and
Hugo was concerned about the spring growth. Jess
listened with half an ear while Paige chattered like a

butcher's magpie and ate chocolate chip cookies like there was no tomorrow.

Paige seemed a different child.

'You're hardly eating any,' Paige complained as the child finished off her third. 'Aren't they delicious?'

'Delicious,' Jess agreed. 'But—' she cast a nervous glance at Niall as if expecting him to disagree with her '—I really have to go.'

She stood and the men stood with her.

'I'll take you out to the car,' Paige said importantly but Niall shook his head.

'Six o'clock, Paige, love,' he told her. 'Time for a bath.'

'But. . .'

'No buts.' Niall pointed to the clock. 'We don't argue about the rules.'

'I'll run it for her,' Hugo said and made his way out to the passage. 'After you, Paige, lass.'

They stumped off down the passage and Jess and Niall were left alone.

'I suppose that seems hard,' Niall told Jess. He hadn't moved from where he'd risen but was watching Jessie's face. 'When Paige first came to us she fought us all the way. It was one long scream to have her do anything. We got over it by writing our schedule up on a noticeboard and sticking to it absolutely. Every night at six Paige knows she has a bath, come hell or high water. It seems to work.'

'I've pulled you out of routine, then.'

'You have at that.' Niall's eyes locked on hers across the table. 'And the hard part is that it seems it's changed things for the better.'

'What do you mean?'

His eyes smiled at her, fatigue in their depths as well as humour. 'Hugo and I have been fighting a losing battle—but all of a sudden we seem to have turned a corner. Since her day with you, Paige has been. . .well, she's been a child again.'

'I'm glad.'

'I don't know whether I am or not,' Niall confessed. 'It seems we were doing the wrong thing, keeping her isolated.'

'I'd guess you weren't,' Jess said softly. 'For a start, Paige's illness must have demanded a period of quiet. Now. . . Now Paige has you as her base and she's finding the world again. With luck she'll go from strength to strength.' She hesitated. 'Her legs. . . How bad are they?'

'They're stronger every day. With luck, and with Geraldine's help, she'll walk without aids. She's been very lucky.'

'I'm glad about that too,' Jess said warmly. 'I'd have hated to have interfered for nothing.'

'You interfered to get a doctor for your precious island.' His eyes watched hers for a reaction.

'That's right. I did.'

Jess agreed with him swiftly. If Niall thought he was goading her to argument he was mistaken. Punctilious courtesy and then fast flight. She took a deep breath. 'Thank you for the coffee, Dr Mountmarche. I must go.'

'I'd like to show you the winery.'

Jess licked suddenly dry lips. 'Some other time. . .'

'Scared?'

Her eyes flashed up to his. 'Y-yes,' she confessed. The word was out before she could stop it.

'Why?' Niall leaned back against the kitchen bench, arms folded, surveying her with interest.

'It's none. . .'

'Of my business?' He smiled. 'You're wrong there, Dr Harvey. You've elected me medical superintendent for the island and, as such, the welfare of every islander is, by definition, my concern. Mental as well as physical. So spill the beans, Dr Harvey.'

'There's nothing to spill.' Jess walked two steps towards the door but Niall was faster than she. He cut her off at the pass—somewhere between table and door.

'I think there is,' he said gently. His hands fell onto

her shoulders and he gripped hard. 'You concern your-self with the well-being of my small daughter, Dr Harvey, but you cut me out like I'm a real threat. My daughter has been frightened of me——but that's fading. She's five years old and not used to a male figure. I can understand her fear. What's your excuse?'

'I don't have one,' Jessie whispered. 'Please. . . Let me go.'

He shook his head. Releasing her shoulders he stood, his body still blocking her path and his dark eyes trying to read hers.

'I don't understand what's driving you, Dr Harvey,' he said slowly. 'You're not an islander. Why, then, did you decide to practise here? It's hardly a profitable veterinary practice.'

'It pays well enough.'

'Does it?' His eyebrows rose in mock surprise. 'I heard the quote you gave Ray Benn for treating his horse. You'd be lucky to cover the cost of the drugs. There isn't any leeway in there for profit.'

'What I charge is my business.'

'But it seems our life is your business,' he said gravely. He held out his hand. 'Come on, Jess. I want to take you round the vineyard.'

Jess looked at his hand. It was an imperative gesture, demanding her to respond. To place her hand in his.

'I don't want to,' she whispered.

'I'm not going to threaten you, Jessie,' Niall said gently and the hand remained outstretched. 'I'm just going to walk you along the rows of grapes and practise saying, "These are shiraz grapes and these my uncle intended last year for dry semillon only the boutris affected area was so large he ended up making noble rot instead"——and generally sounding like a wine-grower extraordinaire. Indulge me, Jess.'

The hand stayed outstretched.

'I. . .' She looked at the hand. 'No.'

'I insist.' Gentle but firm.

To refuse. . . To refuse was almost an impossibility.

'Five. . .five minutes, then.'

'Ten.' His eyes were teasing her and he reached forward to grasp her hand, willing or not. 'Ten minutes of education. It should just about stretch my knowledge to the limit.'

It did no such thing.

The vines covered thirty or so acres of north-facing hillside. Niall walked Jess from row to row, ignoring her reluctance and talking as he went. It didn't take Jess long to realise that Niall Mountmarche knew more than he let on.

Wine-growing was in his blood, he'd told her once, and she knew that it was more than that. This knowledge came from a lifetime of reading and thinking and preparing for a future he wasn't trained for.

'Did you know you'd inherit this place?' she asked curiously as they returned along the rows toward her car. Jessie's hand was still linked in Niall's and the feel of it was doing strange things to her—but she'd recovered her equilibrium enough to find her voice.

'No.' Niall's steady flow of talk cut off. He looked down at her as if he were preparing to say something— and then thought better of it.

'So it came as a surprise.'

'You could say that.'

They drew to a halt by her car.

'Come and see where we do the crushing,' Niall suggested but Jess shook her head.

'My animals need feeding. I've been away for too long already.'

'But you haven't come to any harm spending this time with me,' Niall said gently and Jess flushed.

'Of course not. . .'

She tried pulling her hand away but Niall would have none of it. His hold tightened.

'Jess. . .'

'Let me go, please.'

'I don't think I want to,' he said softly. 'The more I see you the more I believe letting you go would be a

crazy, crazy thing to do. I've only just found you—
and I've never known anything so precious.'

Jessie was silenced.

The sun was low on the horizon, casting a brilliant,
fiery sheen over the sky as it set in crimson glory. The
whole world, it seemed, was holding its breath.

Waiting.

'Please. . .'

'Why are you frightened, Jess?'

'I hardly know you.' It was a tremulous whisper.

'And I hardly know you,' Niall responded. His hand
came up to cup her chin, forcing her eyes up to his.
'But that's hardly true, is it, Jess? Maybe I've known
you in a past life but somewhere—somehow—a link's
been built that's stronger than both of us. I felt it the
first time I saw you—and your fear tells me that you
feel it, too.'

'No. . .'

'Yes.' He didn't let her eyes leave his. 'Jess, why
the fear? What have I ever done to deserve it? I don't
know what I'm fighting here.'

'You're not fighting anything,' Jess stammered.
'Please. . . Let me go.'

'Not until I know. . .' His eyes devoured her face
and his fingers came up to touch her forehead. Above
her eye was the faint trace of an old wound, running
from hair line down to brow.

The tear had been skilfully repaired. It was
hardly noticeable—but Niall Mountmarche had
surgeon's eyes.

'What caused this?' he asked and his voice was
deceptively mild—as if enquiring about the weather.

'Nothing.' Jess pulled angrily away but Niall gripped
and held.

'If it was nothing then you'd tell me,' he said mildly.
'A savage dog? Hardly. No tear marks. It looks like
something's hit you so hard the skin's split. Am
I right?'

'It's nothing.' Jess put her hand up to cover the scar.

She covered it carefully with make-up and normally no one noticed—except this man with the eyes of a hawk.

A hawk with his eyes on his prey.

'Let me go.'

'Tell me, Jess.' The voice was insistent. 'I've a feeling I need to know.'

'You don't.'

'Someone hit you? Is that why you're running scared? Has someone knocked you around in the past?'

The insistent voice was suddenly laced with anger—as though the thought of such a thing was abhorrent.

'No. . .'

'Then tell me.'

'I don't have to.'

'No.' He pulled her into him and bent to kiss the fine line of scarring. 'You don't. But I need to know, my lovely Jess, and if you don't tell me then I'll be forced to resort to other methods. The other doctors on this island? The ones who are doing their training on the mainland. One of them's your cousin, I think you said. I'll find out who he is and contact him if I must—or resort to even deeper stratagems. Would he tell me?'

'You have no right,' she flashed in fury.

'To fight for what I'm starting to think matters most in the world?' Niall shook his head, his hands resisting her furious pull away from his. 'I might not have the right—but I fight to win, Jessica Harvey. And I want to win you.'

'Well, want to your heart's content,' Jess snapped. She put her hands against his chest and shoved for all she was worth. 'Dr Mountmarche, I don't know you. You have a life I know nothing of. You could turn out to be a crook—a murderer for all I know. . .'

'Is that what happened in the past?'

'If you want to know, then, yes,' Jess flung at him. She was trapped in his hold and her voice held desperation. 'I met a lawyer. John Talbot. A nice solid, safe, dependable lawyer. The sort of man my mum would be delighted with if I brought him home for Sunday

lunch. Only he turned out to be a little more than ı
bargained for. He killed a man. . . And when I tried to
go to the law he very nearly killed me.'

'He did this?' Niall touched Jessie's scar with infinite tenderness.

There was no imagining Niall Mountmarche's
anger now. This man was one who would protect his
own, Jess thought, and for one fleeting moment she
let herself imagine how it would feel to be Niall
Mountmarche's woman.

She would be no man's woman. She had determined
that. She wanted no man near her unless she had known
them since birth—known their every movement
through life.

She couldn't trust again. There had been more than
Jess hurt last time because of her crazy trust. She had
trusted a man who was a drug dealer, a thief and a
murderer and not only had he tried to kill her but he'd
come close to killing her friends as well.

It was a lesson well learned.

The only problem was that Niall Mountmarche was
standing before her, demanding her trust with every
ounce of will in his body.

Niall Mountmarche was different, her wilful heart
screamed at her.

This man wasn't such a one as John Talbot. How
could he be? He'd left his medical practice to rescue
his small daughter and bring her a world away from
his career in London. John Talbot would hardly have
done that. John Talbot looked out for John Talbot. Only
for John Talbot.

So maybe she could trust.

Maybe she could follow her heart. . .

'No matter what that bastard did to you,' Niall said
strongly, his hands catching hers and holding firm, 'it
doesn't affect us, Jess. What's between us. . .it's
special. Unique. You felt it the same as I when we met
for the first time. I thought you were a child trespassing
on my land—and you. . .' He smiled his caress of a

smile that made Jessie's heart do handstands. 'You thought of me as the Ogre of Barega. And yet what was between us grew. It has a life of its own. Trust it, Jess. Trust me.'

'I can't. . .' Jessie's voice was a frightened whisper and her face drained of colour.

'Why not?'

'You don't know. . .'

'What he did to you?' There was a stillness in Niall's eyes. He met her frightened look and he swore.

'Where is he now, Jess?'

'In. . .in prison.'

'May he rot there,' Niall said savagely. 'Jess, give me a chance.'

'I can't.'

'You can,' he said softly. 'All you have to do is trust. Put your heart in my keeping, my lovely Jessie, and watch how I treasure it. I swear. . .'

'Niall, don't. . .' Jess pulled away. 'Please, it's too soon. It's too. . .I hardly know you. I. . .I've known you less than a week. . .'

'So you have,' Niall said slowly, his eyes never leaving her face. 'Less than a week. Why do I feel as if you've been in my heart for all of my life?'

'No!' It was a cry of panic. Things were way out of control here.

She never should have let this go so far. She had to get away. 'Please, Niall. . .'

'Let you go?' He released her then and stepped back. The smile faded from his eyes.

'I can't constrain you, Jessie,' he said softly. 'I can't make you trust me. I can only hope. . .'

'No. . . Please. . . I have to go. . .'

Silence.

Then, very slowly as if acknowledging some absolute truth, Niall Mountmarche nodded.

'You do.' Niall looked at his wrist-watch and gave rueful smile. 'Your responsibilities await, my lovely

Jessie. But wherever you go, know that your hea
rests here.'

He didn't touch her again. Jess stood stock still,
staring up at him with frightened eyes.

Did she dare trust?

Dear heaven. . .

'I have to go,' she whispered again and, with a sob
of panic, she turned and fled.

CHAPTER EIGHT

It was a strange and stressful week.

Jessie's working world had changed dramatically.

The little hospital seemed to come alive. It was as if it had been hibernating—waiting. Niall Mountmarche's presence was everywhere.

The nurses thought Dr Mountmarche wonderful— and so did the islanders. They arrived at the clinic in droves, driven more by curiosity than ill health, and Niall found himself booked solid.

'What on earth have you got me into?' he laughed at Jess as they passed in the corridor toward the end of the week—and Jess flinched.

'I'm sorry. . .I never meant. . .'

'To drag me or my daughter out of hibernation?' He barred her passage and laughed down into her tense face. 'Liar. You've lost the island its ogre.'

'I'm. . .'

Her voice faded. This man made her feel totally inept.

'How's Matilda?' Niall's smile faded.

'Not. . .not good.' Jess took a deep breath. She was behaving like a nervous kid—and, for heaven's sake, this man was a medical colleague. 'I think we're losing the battle.'

'I'm sorry to hear that,' Niall said gently and his eyes told her that his words weren't just a platitude. He knew how much Matilda meant to the Benns.

'She's still standing,' Jess told him, her voice unconsciously forlorn, 'but. . .'

'But?'

She shrugged. 'It's a big "but".' She hesitated. The thought of Matilda as she'd last seen her depressed her unutterably.

119

Try another topic.

'Wasn't Paige meant to be with me this afternoon?' The informal arrangement was that Paige would spend most of her days with Jess but more and more the child was immersing herself in hospital life. At any given time she could be with one of the nurses or making biscuits with Cook or chatting to the hospital gardener. As long as she knew where Jess and Niall were the little girl seemed content.

'Listen for the giggles and you'll find her,' Niall smiled. 'If it wasn't for my daughter I'd be cursing your interference but. . .'

'A happier "but"?' Jess asked and smiled.

'A happier "but". Jessie, I'd like you to come to the vineyard for dinner tonight.'

'I'm busy.'

'Doing?'

'Doing what I need to do,' Jess snapped. She took a deep breath. 'Dr Mountmarche, my little animals need feeding and I have to go back out to the Benns.'

'Ask Geraldine's daughter to feed your babies.'

'I might have to, anyway,' Jess admitted. 'Matilda's really getting worse. Tonight. . .'

'Could be the end?' Niall's eyes showed concern. 'That bad, Jess?'

'That bad.'

'Would you like me to come with you?'

'No.' Jess shook her head. 'I can cope alone.'

'You always do—but you don't have to.'

'Yes, I do,' Jessie said blankly. 'Now. . . If you'll excuse me. . .'

'Let me close, Jess,' Niall said softly and it was as much as Jessie could do not to burst into tears.

'N-no,' she managed again—but only just—and turned and walked in the opposite direction.

Niall couldn't have helped.

Jess tried to make her confused mind get things straight as she drove out to the Benns.

Niall Mountmarche was laying siege to her heart. Somehow he'd penetrated the armour she'd so carefully built in the year since she'd been betrayed and nearly killed by John Talbot. Just by looking at her, Niall Mountmarche could pierce her shell-like armour.

The shell was a fragile protection.

So. . .

So grow thicker armour, she snapped to herself savagely as she drove into the night. Or run. . .

There's nowhere to run.

You could leave the island.

Some things were unthinkable.

'I can't face it.'

There was more than one thing that was unthinkable.

Jess faced Ray Benn with a heavy heart. The man had been waiting for her. He swung back the gate and, as she emerged from the car, Jess saw his broad face was streaked with tears.

'She's down, Jess. . . Her legs just folded on her a couple of hours ago. I can't. . . I dunno. . . I just can't bear to watch. She's suffered enough.'

Jess put a gentle hand on his shoulder. 'I'll do what I must, Ray,' she told him. 'You wait inside.'

There was little enough to do. Jess knelt in the stall with the ailing mare and ran her hand along the trembling flank. This was a cruel way for a horse to end her days—all for want of simple vaccination.

There was nothing Jess could do to save her now. Once a horse this ill was down. . .

She gave the injection fast and Matilda died quietly on the straw.

It was over. . .

Jess walked slowly back into the house and found the family in tears. The whole family. Mum, Dad and six children. Even the baby was wailing, though Jess wouldn't mind betting that he didn't know what for.

'I'll arrange for someone to collect Matilda's body

in the morning,' she said helplessly and set off a fresh paroxysm of sobs.

'We'll bury her here, lass,' Ray told her through choked-back tears. 'This is her home.'

There was nothing more for Jessie to do. Helplessly she packed her bags and beat a retreat. Ray followed her out to the car.

'You know what's really getting me?' he said. 'We didn't keep any of her foals. The last foal she had was a little beauty. The kids begged me to keep her—but horses cost money and I said no. Now I wish. . .' He rubbed a grimy hand across wet cheeks and sniffed. 'Eh, well. . .'

If the other fishermen could see Ray Benn now they'd be astounded, Jess thought as she retired back into her little car. A tough male—with a marshmallow middle.

It was enough to make her want to weep herself.

The death of the mare stayed with her all the way home. The hospital was quiet. Frank had taken Harry home that morning. Niall had admitted a child with asthma but Geraldine was coping competently—and by the sound of it the child slept.

Niall and Paige must have gone back to the vineyard.

Jess fed her little animals, then sat on the floor and talked to them for a while. Bed seemed unutterably lonely.

Ten o'clock on a Friday night.

Nothing in front of her but lonely bed.

Don't be so stupid, she told herself savagely. Nothing but bed! What else do you want, for heaven's sake? Someone to share your bed with you? You have to be crazy.

She was definitely crazy.

Yes! her heart was screaming for all it was worth. That's exactly what she wanted. Someone to share. . .

Someone?

She wanted Niall.

Jess went drearily to bed but she couldn't sleep.

If she'd accepted Niall Mountmarche's invitation she could be out at the vineyard right this minute, drinking coffee by the fire and watching Niall Mountmarche smile. . .

'You're a stupid, senseless twit,' she said savagely into the night and it was as much as Jess could do not to burst into tears like the Benns.

The phone rang an hour after she turned off her lights.

Jess groped in the darkness for the phone, swore as she knocked over the lamp and had to fumble on the floor for the light switch. She finally picked up the receiver on the tenth ring.

'Yes?'

'Problem, Jess.' It was the clipped voice of Sergeant Russell.

Jess sat up, her confusion fading. If Sergeant Russell said that there was a problem, there always was.

'How can I help?'

'I've a domestic out at the Simmonses'. It seems Ethel and Barry are having a go at each other—again— but it's got a bit out of hand. They're both injured and that damned mutt of Ethel's—you know the Rottweiler?—won't let anyone near her. Can you come?'

'I'll come. How badly are they hurt?'

'I don't know,' the sergeant admitted. 'All I know is Barry's unconscious and I can't get near Ethel. I've called Doc Mountmarche and he's on his way. The sooner you're both here the happier I'll be.'

'Give me five minutes.'

Jess dressed fast, pulling on jeans, sweater and leather shoes. She grabbed leather gloves from the wardrobe and considered.

She had a flexi-rod which usually enabled her to handle aggressive dogs—a rod with a loop at one end which, when slipped over the dog's head, could be tightened fast, thus holding the dog at more than teeth's reach from the handler.

Maybe. . .

She thought—and then packed tranquilliser and a couple of barbs. In a case like this, a tranquilliser dart might be more effective.

There was an hour to go before her two little animals were due to be fed and they were getting stronger every day. If they missed one night feed it wouldn't kill them.

OK.

She took a deep breath, the adrenalin surging at the thought of what lay ahead. At the thought that somewhere out in the night Niall Mountmarche would be gearing up for the same emergency as Jess.

Niall Mountmarche has nothing to do with the way I'm feeling, she said to herself crossly as she made her way out to the car.

Liar.

Niall Mountmarche had everything to do with it.

He beat her to the Simmonses'.

The Simmonses lived in a ramshackle house on the edge of town. It was a dump. There was rubbish—everything from last week's shopping bags to a couple of old car bodies—strewn around the grounds.

Mrs Simmons was a good-hearted woman who'd been walked all over by an aggressive husband in the thirty years of their marriage. Jess had seen a little of her. She kept a horse in stables at the rear of the house and many times Jess suspected that she spent the housekeeping money on her horse and her dog—not herself. The woman looked as if she was suffering from malnutrition.

Ethel had given up on keeping either herself or her home presentable.

Barry Simmons wasn't suffering from the same malnutrition as his wife. Barry was heavily overweight, mostly brought on by too much booze. He was supposed to be a fisherman but his evil temper meant that he was now almost unemployable.

He was hardly one of Jessie's favourite people.

So what had happened tonight?

Jess pulled up on the road outside the Simmonses'. The police car had its lights shining directly at the house and the flashing light on top of the car was still beaming iridescent blue. The ambulance was parked behind it. Niall had decided the vehicle was more use staying with him and had taken it back to the vineyard. He must have driven it here.

The house itself was in darkness, though there seemed to be a lantern of some sort glinting close to the front door. A couple of neighbours were standing well back from the house, whispering among themselves. They watched Jess from a safe distance, their stance proclaiming clearly their desire to remain uninvolved.

From the house came low, menacing growls. Ethel's dog?

Why wasn't the Rottweiler outside?

Where was everyone?

Jess collected her gear and picked her way cautiously through the rubbish-strewn yard—keeping a weather eye out for stray Rottweilers as she went. A huge black shadow launching itself at her throat from the darkness was hardly a great way to spend a night.

Or to end a night. . .

She didn't make it to the front door. As soon as Jess passed the worst of the overgrown garden she found where the action was. To the left, against the wall of the building and behind a tangle of bushes, was Barry Simmons, Sergeant Russell—and Niall.

Barry Simmons looked dead.

Jess stared down at his unconscious form. What on earth had happened?

There was a chainsaw lying on the ground and a gaping, jagged hole sawn roughly from the wall of the house.

'Sergeant Russell?' Jess said tentatively and the policeman glanced up from Barry Simmons's inert form and clambered speedily to his feet.

'Jess. . . Thank God you're here.' It sounded as though he really meant it.

'What's happened?' Jess stared down to where Niall was working on the prone body of Barry Simmons. The big man was sprawled limply on the grass, his massive frame unmoving.

'He's alive,' the policeman said quickly. 'He's drunk as a skunk, though, Jess——and Doc Mountmarche reckons he's electrocuted himself.'

'Electrocuted. . .'

Niall looked up then, his expression drawn and grim in the light of the lantern beside him.

'His pulse is strong enough, Jess. There's a nasty burn on one hand——but nothing that should kill him. It's my guess it's alcohol that's keeping him knocked out.'

'But what happened?' Jess asked again. She stared at the hole in the wall. Here was Ethel's Rottweiler. The big dog was staring out through the jagged cavity, snarling at all of them. If he wished he could lunge at any minute.

He could take a piece out of any one of them.

'The neighbours say there was a huge domestic earlier tonight,' the policeman told her, keeping one eye firmly fixed on the dog. 'It seems Ethel locked Barry out. Barry went down to the pub, got himself tanked and came home to a locked house.' He gestured to the hole in the wall. 'So he thought of a brand-new way of getting into a locked house.'

'By chainsaw?' Jess asked incredulously.

'By chainsaw. Chop a ruddy great hole in your wife's bedroom wall. And while you're doing it, chop through the electric wiring as well.'

'Clever.' Jess looked down at the dog. 'Is there live wiring in the hole?'

'We turned the electricity off to the whole place. The service people are on their way.'

Jess looked again at the dog——and then down at Niall. 'How can I help?' she asked him.

Niall shrugged and rose. 'Give us a suggestion about

the dog.' He looked down at Barry with an expression of distaste on his face. 'Barry'll live—whether he deserves to or not after such a damned fool stunt. I need to see Ethel.'

'She's still inside?'

'She's been hurt,' Niall told her, 'but I don't know how badly. Sergeant Russell shone his flashlight through the window. She's in there and she's alive. He saw her move—but she's on the floor and she's not responding. We can't get in because of the dog.'

'I could shoot the mutt,' Sergeant Russell said grimly. 'Not through the hole in the wall—that would risk putting a bullet into Ethel—but if we break the window then I could get a bullet into the dog before it took a piece out of me. But. . .'

'But Ethel loves her dog,' Jess protested gently. 'And it's done nothing wrong. It's been trained to protect her and that's what it's doing. She won't want it dead, as well as everything else that's happened to her.'

'Too bad if she's bleeding to death.'

'Can you see if she's bleeding?'

'No.' The policeman shook his head. 'I can't see much at all. We daren't turn the electricity on again to give us power.'

'The electricity can't have killed her,' Niall told Jess, 'if she was moving afterwards. . .'

'She looked like she was crawling back behind the bed when I saw her,' the policeman explained. 'I called out to her and she just sort of went limp. And then nothing. . .'

'Where's the window?' Jess asked.

She looked closely at the dog's snarling face through the hole, considering her options. To snare the dog with the flexi-rod through the hole in the wall was almost an impossibility. The dog just had to move back every time the rod went near—and as for clambering through the hole. . .

Not with those waiting teeth.

'Round the side.' The policeman took Jessie's bag. 'After you, Doc.'

'Hurry, Jess,' Niall said quietly. 'Shoot if necessary. If Ethel's had a solid shock then maybe her heart's given out. . .'

Jess went.

Thirty seconds later Jess was shining a torch through the window into the darkened bedroom.

There was very little to see. There was a crumpled form on the bare floor, half hidden by the bed. The dog was still bristling and snarling through the hole in the wall but directing the odd nervous glance in the direction of the torch's beam.

Nothing else. . .

'If I went into the house through the door I'd have to kill the dog,' the policeman said nervously. 'And at that close range I'm not at all sure I'd kill it before it had a good go at me.'

'No.' Jess shook her head. 'You'd be asking for trouble. But if we broke the top pane of the window the dog couldn't reach.'

'And?'

Jess bent down, fumbling in her bag. 'Tranquilliser dart,' she said briefly. 'My favourite toy. I use them to tranquillise wild animals—for instance, if I need to transport a full grown kangaroo or give it antibiotics. If I can just aim it right. . .' She loaded the dart and looked up at Sergeant Russell's broad shoulders. 'Can I stand on you?'

He grinned. 'I knew there was a reason we had a nice slender girl vet.' He looked behind Jess to where Niall had appeared. 'Ready to give us a hand, Doc?'

'I'm ready. Barry's stable,' Niall said briefly. 'His breathing's regular. I'd rather send him to the lock-up than the hospital—there'll be a fair mess when he wakes, at a guess. I can dress his hand at the lock-up.'

'Gee, thanks,' the policeman grimaced. Then his frown deepened as a steady groan came from where

Barry had been left. It seemed that he was emerging from his drunken stupor.

'I'd go back and keep him under control if I were you, Sergeant,' Niall said blandly. 'There's no guarantee he won't pick up the chainsaw and keep slicing. If we hadn't turned off the electricity he could kill the lot of us.'

Sergeant Russell swore. He looked from Niall to Jess.

'You can cope here?'

'We can cope,' Niall assured him. 'Just keep bully boy out of our way. Now, Jess, what do you want done?'

Two minutes later the problem was solved.

Niall smashed the pane from the top window, cleared the broken glass and lifted Jess high so that she could see.

It was a weird feeling—to perch on Niall Mountmarche's shoulders. He held her effortlessly, moving not an inch as she carefully aimed her dart gun.

The dog was moving back and forth from hole to smashed window, frantic with anxiety. Jessie's heart went out to the big animal. He might be vicious but he believed that someone was trying to hurt his mistress.

Niall could see through the lower pane. He held the torch unwaveringly on the animal's body as it paced back and forth.

Jess could shoot the dark about eight feet. It was just a matter of waiting until the dog paused. If she could just place the dart where she wanted in the dim light. . .

'Here, boy,' she called as he paced away from them. 'Come on. . . Over here. . .'

The dog launched himself against the window and than sank back, bewildered as he realised that he couldn't reach Jessie's high perch. For ten long seconds he stood, trying to figure out his next move.

Jess raised the dart to her lips, took careful aim at the dog's broad flank and blew.

The dart sank home right on target.

It took moments to work.

The dog snarled, backed away, snarled some more—and then staggered.

It tried another half-hearted growl but its body wasn't working to command. The dog took three uncertain steps backwards—and then crumpled to the floor.

'Great shot.' Niall swung her down and his hands lingered for a fraction more time than was strictly necessary. 'Remind me to stay on your good side, Dr Harvey. Tranquilliser dart—a girl's best friend!' He flashed Jess a swift smile that made her heart miss a beat, then put his hand inside the broken pane, flicked the latch and lifted the bottom window pane.

Ten seconds later they were in the room.

Niall went straight to the woman beside the bed, leaving Jess to follow. She didn't follow immediately. Jess took seconds to muzzle the dog and clip a short lead from his collar to the bedpost. She'd given him minimal dosage and she didn't want him waking.

Finally, she joined Niall.

'What. . .?'

'Trouble,' Niall said briefly. He'd rolled Ethel Simmons into the recovery position and his hands were moving swiftly over her. 'We're dealing with major blood loss, I think.'

'But. . .'

Then Jess saw what Niall had found and she drew in her breath in horror.

Ethel's right hand was a bloody, mangled mess. She'd lost a finger—two, maybe—and the rest of her hand was sliced and crushed.

'It's my guess she had her hand on the wall when the chainsaw came through,' Niall said grimly. 'If she was yelling at him not to be so stupid—and he shoved the thing through, anyway. . .'

Niall was searching Ethel's arm for pressure points. 'Jess, in the ambulance there's saline and there's morphine in my bag. There's a burn here—look—she got shocked the same as her husband. There must be circuit breakers on the power supply or they'd both be dead.'

'She's not. . .?'

'There's still a pulse—faint. No, she's not dead. Go, Jess. . .'

Jess went.

Outside, the yard had come alive. The electricity servicemen had arrived and set up huge floodlights to show them what they were dealing with. Jess grabbed what she needed, threw orders for stretcher bearers and returned at a run.

She worked beside Niall in silence, concentrating fiercely on anticipating his needs.

He had the pressure points.

'Take over here, Jess,' he ordered in the same clinical tone he'd use for a theatre nurse. 'Press down here—hard. If the bleeding restarts then you're not pressing hard enough.'

With Jessie controlling the bleeding, Niall was free for other things. In minutes he had the worst of the bleeding staunched by pressure bandage, a drip set up and morphine administered into Ethel's limp body.

Still the woman didn't stir.

How badly had she been electrocuted? It couldn't have been lethal if she'd moved afterwards.

'Blood pressure about ninety on fifty.' Niall swore. 'And dropping. We're going to need some plasma fast. I'll radio ahead to Geraldine to prepare for cross-matching.'

He looked up then, assessing his manpower.

'OK, let's move her,' Niall said swiftly. There were men crowding into the room behind them and he snapped a warning.

'Watch your feet,' he told them. 'Don't move until you see what you're standing on. There are two fingers missing—and if they're intact they might be salvageable. Find some ice in the refrigerator and bring them down to the hospital after us. Jess, I need you to come. Now.'

They shifted Ethel's slight weight to the stretcher

and Jess followed the bearers back into the night. As she went she cast a sympathetic glance at the dog.

'There's a kennel out the back,' she told the men remaining. 'Carry the dog out, tie him up and remove the muzzle before he wakes. Make sure he has plenty of water available. I'll decide what needs to be done for him in the morning.'

There was nothing more she could do for the dog.

There was only Ethel.

The fingers were unsalvageable.

The men found remains of them spattered onto the chainsaw. They brought them down to the hospital and Niall inspected them in grim silence as Jess and Geraldine prepared Theatre.

'Non-viable,' he said bitterly. 'Damn. . .'

The surgery was difficult enough, anyway.

Jess gave the anaesthetic—a role she'd learned as the island's vet. One doctor and one vet on the island meant that the only option was to give anaesthetics for each other's patients in emergencies, despite genetic differences.

'It's only learning about one more sort of animal,' Jess had joked to her cousin the first time she'd been asked to do it—but it was more than that. Human life was infinitely precious—and infinitely complex. . .

And Ethel was frail at the best of times.

Jess concentrated fiercely on Niall's instructions as he debrided the wound and tied off slashed blood vessels.

Niall operated as if he was completely at home at the operating table and Jess had the feeling that he was competent to deal with worse dramas than the one he was dealing with here.

He took Jessie's lack of human experience on board without a murmur, swiftly assessing how much she knew and didn't know and changing his own role accordingly. His fingers moved swiftly and skilfully—and

Jess was sure that she was looking at something other than basic general practice training.

'I thought you were a GP,' she said bluntly and Niall smiled.

'Well, I guess I am,' he agreed. 'Or was. But I'm also a surgeon.'

'I. . .I see. . .'

Jess didn't see at all. There were things about this man that she could only guess at.

She couldn't guess at them now, though. There was too much else to concentrate on.

To Niall's and Jessie's relief Ethel had stirred from unconsciousness briefly before going under anaesthetic—but had welcomed the anaesthetic like a friend.

There was no joy for her in consciousness.

Geraldine crossmatched blood as they worked, leaving Jess as the only assistant. Ethel needed unit after unit of blood.

'She's so thin,' Niall muttered as he operated. 'There are no reserves. Tell me about her, Jess.'

'What do you want to know?' Jess was concentrating totally on the task at hand. She hardly heard the question.

'What sort of woman are we operating on?'

Jess forced herself to think.

'A pathetic one,' she said at last. 'Barry knocks her round—it's common knowledge on the island. She doesn't have enough money for the basic necessities.' Jess paused as she concentrated on her row of dials and then started again. 'Barry drinks all the little money he earns—and most of hers. She takes in ironing and does other people's housework.'

'There are bruises here not caused by any chainsaw.'

Jess nodded. 'That doesn't surprise me.'

'Has anyone talked to her about leaving him?'

'I have.' Jess had agonised over intervening the first few times she'd met the haunted, softly spoken woman but had finally decided that she couldn't ignore Ethel's cringing every time her husband was mentioned.

'Last time her dog was vaccinated I had to stitch the dog's shoulder where Barry had planted a boot—and Ethel had bruises which looked worse.' Jess shrugged. 'I didn't achieve much. It's a huge thing for Ethel to walk away from her husband. She married him thirty years ago when she was sixteen. Her children have long since left the island because of Barry's evil temper.'

'Well, she's not going to get a lot older if she stays with him, that's for sure.' Niall sighed and straightened. 'Reverse please, Jess.' He moved position to assist her. 'I've done all I can—but she needs a trip to the mainland.'

'For plastic surgery?'

'They can rebuild her thumb. By the look of the wear on her hands she's left-handed and she'll be lost without the thumb. With clever grafting they'll shift a toe—if she agrees.'

'A toe. . .'

'Big toes are extraneous,' he smiled wearily. 'Missing thumbs are a real pest. We'll give her the choice in the morning. But for now. . .for now. . .'

For now Ethel needed to sleep. She lay shrunken and pallid on the trolley as she started to breathe normally and Jessie's heart went out to her.

'What about Barry?' she asked as Geraldine wheeled Ethel out into the ward and Niall and Jess removed their gowns at the sink.

'I'll go to the lock-up now,' Niall told her. 'I'd prefer to dress his hand there. Sergeant Russell will keep him under observation for the night—and I'd rather have him making a fuss out of earshot of Ethel.'

'I'd like to know why she locked him out.'

'Some of those bruises are recent,' Niall said grimly. 'And by the look of her arm I'd say there's a break that hasn't been set properly. If I had to guess I'd say the lady's been living in fear for quite a while.' He sighed. 'I'll go now and dress Barry's hand and come back. . .'

'You'll stay here the night?'

'I'd rather be close until Ethel's stabilised,' he said. 'Paige will be right with Hugo. Ethel's fairly trauma-tised—and she's lost a lot of blood.'

Jess nodded. 'I'll. . .I'll go to bed, then,' she told him softly. 'I'll see you in the morning.'

'You do that,' he smiled and touched her face lightly with one finger. 'You do that.'

CHAPTER NINE

BED. . .

Not yet. First there were her two little orphans.

For Jess there were always her two—or more—little orphans. They were restless when she got back to her flat, the little wallaby out of his pouch and nosing around the kitchen. Jess sat on the floor by the stove and gave them their milk, using the time to settle her jangled nerves.

She should relax. . .

She couldn't.

Niall was gone. He was down at the police station attending the awful Barry.

So. . .

If Niall was gone why were her senses alight as though electrified? Her whole body seemed to be straining—listening for his return.

He'd go straight to his flat, she told herself crossly. There was no reason for him to come past her room.

He'd check Ethel again.

He could come this way.

It didn't matter if he did. He'd just walk straight down the corridor, check Ethel, keep going, turn left and go to his side of the hospital.

Right.

So she should get into bed and not sit here by the fire nursing stupid wallabies and listening for stupid footsteps.

'I'm going nuts,' she told the little wallaby, and the tiny animal looked up as though in complete agreement.

A car.

The ambulance returning from the police station.

Footsteps down the corridor. They checked outside Ethel's room. Paused. Stayed for ten minutes. There

136

was a low conversation at the ward door as Niall gave Geraldine her instructions for the night.

The footsteps came on.

Down the corridor and turn left.

Down the corridor. . .

They didn't turn left. The footsteps stopped right outside Jessie's door.

She was hardly breathing. Somehow her lungs had stopped—or was it her heart?

'Jess?' A light tap on the door—not loud enough to be heard by Geraldine. 'Awake?'

No. She shouldn't be awake. She should be inside her bed with the bedroom door locked and with chains on her heart.

Instead of which she was placing the tiny wallaby on the floor and crossing to open the door.

'Niall. . .'

'Who did you think it was?' he asked wickedly. 'Santa Claus?'

'It might have been a call,' she said with quiet dignity. 'I do get them.'

'Surely your farmers don't come scratching on your bedroom door at three in the morning?' he teased. He took a step into the room but paused as Jess laid a warning hand on his arm. 'What's wrong?'

'Wilfred's out,' she said briefly. 'Watch your feet.'

'Wilfred?' Niall looked around—and then down. His eyes creased into a smile at the sight of the little wallaby nosing his shoes. 'Wilfred,' he said in satisfaction, leaning over and scooping the joey into his large hand. 'Haven't you heard it's time youngsters were in bed?'

'He's a nocturnal animal,' Jess smiled, moving aside to let Niall come closer to the fire. 'In another month or so I'll be starting to prepare him for release.'

'How do you do that?'

'I put him out on the verandah at first,' Jess told him. She was having trouble making her voice work. Niall's presence filled the room.

'He learns to come and go as he pleases. I start weaning him off milk. When he's thoroughly weaned I move his pouch out near the back fence and start putting pellets on both sides of the boundary. The wild wallabies come in to feed—and Wilfred feeds alongside them, with the fence between them. After a few months I open the gate at night so that the wild wallabies can come in—or Wilfred can go out.'

'It's a long process,' Niall said thoughtfully.

'Any faster and the wild animals will kill him,' Jess said. 'After he's acclimatised I go back to laying pellets further from the fence on the outer side of the boundary—I'm doing that now—so animals I've already released always have a fall-back position.' She smiled. 'So they're released—but I usually keep track of them for ever. That's the plan, at any rate.'

'For ever,' Niall said slowly. 'That's a long time, Jess.'

'I'm in no hurry,' she said equably. Then, at the look on Niall's face, her composure left her. 'How. . .how was Barry?'

'Aggressive. Belligerent. Foul-mouthed. Called his wife every name in the book—and a few more besides. Sergeant Russell ended up charging him with assault so we can keep him locked up and I don't have to admit him here.'

'Can you do that?' Jess said doubtfully. 'If he was on the other side of the wall then he wouldn't know where Ethel's hand was.'

'I'm not saying tonight was any more than a stupid, mindless accident,' Niall told her. 'But there's the bruising, the unset broken arm and your evidence.'

'She won't lay charges.'

'My evidence will hold him until she's fit to decide whether to lay charges or not,' Niall said in satisfaction. 'I've given her a fair dose of pethidine now with orders that it be repeated two-hourly. If she doesn't need pain relief she sure as heck needs a sedative. She's been through a shocking experience. The lady will sleep—

or will be reported to be sleeping—until we can arrange an air ambulance to the mainland. It might have to wait until she's in Sydney before the police interview her. With luck Barry might have to kick his heels in the lock-up for two days.'

'You and Sergeant Russell thought that up,' Jess accused and Niall grinned.

'We're just following the law. And sometimes the law is a very handy thing. And very, very slow.'

'I see.'

Jessie's answering smile was unsure. She lifted her little wallaby and held him close. Niall stood smiling down at her and she felt shy—and infinitely vulnerable. 'Well, thank. . .thank you for coming to tell me. I'll. . .I'll put Wilfred to bed now.'

'I didn't come to tell you anything,' Niall said softly and the smile on his face changed. He put a hand out and touched the soft fur of the wallaby. 'I came to see you. And Wilfred doesn't want to go to bed.'

'He does. . .'

'I think it's your duty as Wilfred's treating veterin-arian to introduce him to his new life,' Niall smiled. 'And as the island's new medical superintendent it's my duty to superintend you while you superintend Wilfred.'

'I. . .I beg your pardon.'

'We're going for a walk,' Niall told her. His hand dropped to take hers in a grip that brooked no argument. 'You're still dressed, I see. Wise girl.' He smiled again and his smile made Jessie's heart do strange things inside her. 'Did you know I'd come back, then? Or hope. . .?'

'I did no such thing,' Jess managed with an attempt at dignity. 'I. . .I had to feed my animals.'

'For close on an hour?' He shook his head and gently led her over to the outside door. 'Sweet liar,' he whispered and ushered her outside into the moonlight.

It was a night of magic.

The moon hung low over the horizon, glinting across

the distant sea. Jess was wearing a soft sweater over her jeans but she hardly needed it. The warmth of the night was comfort enough.

The smell of the sea was in the air and the fragrant stands of Australian native frangipani were dropping a scattering of creamy yellow blooms in the breeze drifting from the ocean.

There were fuchsias growing in profusion by the verandah. Jess placed the tiny joey gently on the green grass and the joey took one look at the fuchsia bushes and started to munch. Heaven for a small wallaby. . .

He'd make it, Jess thought in satisfaction. This little one followed his instincts—and he was coming through his tough times.

He followed his instincts. . .

A dangerous path.

Jess glanced sideways at Niall Mountmarche's dark figure and her heart misgave her.

Should she too be following her instincts?

Along what dangerous path were her instincts leading her?

She shouldn't be out here. She should gather her little wallaby and run.

'I know who looks like the wild creature here,' Niall said conversationally. He stood with his hands in his pockets, surveying Jess and her joey with satisfaction. 'You look like something's about to eat you. If I had to guess which of you was more afraid. . .'

'Wilfred hasn't learned to be afraid yet,' Jess whispered.

'And you have?'

'Y-yes.'

'There's no need.' Niall moved then, once more swinging into that lithe, easy movement which reminded Jess of a big cat. Effortless. . .

Jess couldn't move. She was like a small creature in his sights—powerless to resist.

And not sure that she wanted to.

'Jess, don't look like that. . .'

He gathered her hands, pulling her body into his in a swift, sure movement. 'Jess, there's no need for fear. There can't be. I've spent my life looking for someone like you—and I'd started to think she didn't exist.'

'No. . . Please. . .'

'There's no "no" about it, my Jessie,' he murmured. 'Here you are, my lovely, lovely Jess, and I need you to say "yes" more than I need life itself. My Jess of wild creatures. You've come into my life and lifted my daughter from her cage of fear. You've pulled me from the shadows and bullied me into medicine again.

'You. . .you take the whole world on your shoulders—and yet you fear it. There's sanctuary for the healer as well, Jess, if only. . .if only you'll let me into your heart.'

'I can't. . . I don't. . .' Jessie's face was against the coarse cotton of his shirt. She could feel his heart beat—strong and sure.

'You don't what?' He put her away from him, holding her at arm's length and watching her face in the moonlight. 'You trusted one man once—one man out of many—and that one man betrayed you. Are you going to impose John Talbot's face on mine—see him wherever you see me? I'm here to tell you, Jess, that love has nothing to do with what was between you and John Talbot. Love has no fear.' His grip tightened. 'Except. . .except the fear of losing.'

'Niall. . .'

'I swear to you, Jess,' he said softly. 'I have no hidden agenda. There are no vicious surprises in my background. I want you for your own lovely self.'

'You. . .'

'I want *you*, Jess,' he said, his voice low and husky with emotion. She was somehow pulled against him again, his lips moving in her hair. 'I've never wanted anyone. . .' He sighed.

'That sounds false, doesn't it? I've had women before, Jess. You know that. Paige is living proof. I thought. . .I thought I was in love with Paige's

mother—so much so that I asked her to marry me.
Thank God Karen knew better than both of us that the
love wouldn't last. It wasn't the real thing. What I felt
for Karen is a pale shadow of what I'm feeling for one
lovely vet with a heart bigger than any person I've ever
met before.'

His hands moved to her waist, caressing her body
against his.

'I need you, Jess,' he said humbly. 'With a heart
so big, my lovely Jess, can you find a place for me
in there?'

The sureness had gone from his voice. There was a
tremor of uncertainty—as if, for once in his life, Niall
Mountmarche was unsure.

Desperately unsure.

It moved Jess as nothing else could have done. Not
the feel of his hands on her body, the sound of his
voice. . .the steady beating of his heart. . .

She looked up into his face and almost unconsciously
her hands went up to touch. . .to hold. . .to draw his
mouth down to her lips. . .

How could she resist? How could she refuse this
man—this man who was becoming part of her being?
It was as if she was melting into his soul.

'Niall. . .'

And then there was nothing else, except the soft
rustle of the breeze in the frangipani and the distant
murmur of the sea.

Niall's lips met hers and Jessie's doubts drifted off
on the night wind. . .

Somehow. . .sometime and who knew when?—certainly not the lovers—they drew apart. Wilfred had
finished his munching and the joey was huddled uncer-
tainly at Jessie's feet.

Jess gave a shaken gasp and leaned down to scoop
her baby into her arms.

'He should. . . He should be in his bed. . .' she
whispered.

'What a good idea.' Niall's arms linked around her waist enfolding girl and baby wallaby to him in a protective clasp. 'I'll take you both to bed. . .'

'Niall. . .'

'Are you saying you don't want me to take you to your bed, my Jessie?' Niall kissed her lightly on the brow.

'I don't. . . We can't. . .' Jess fought frantically for some trace of common sense. 'Niall, I'm not. . .I'm not protected. . .'

He smiled and his smile was tenderness itself. He kissed her softly on the nose—and then again on the lips. 'There's no use me acting as hospital pharmacist if I can't find what we need in a crisis,' he smiled. He kissed her again, more deeply, like a man becoming addicted to something exquisitely sweet. Infinitely precious. 'And if this isn't a crisis I don't know what is.'

'But. . .' It was all too fast. Too sudden. And yet, to send him away was unthinkable.

'I don't. . .' she whispered and her voice wouldn't utter the words. Jessie was drifting in a haze of unreality. Her heart was close to bursting and she could feel the pinpricks of tears behind her eyes. The long years of loneliness were over, her heart was singing. She had found her home.

'If you don't want me. . . If you don't want me tonight then I'll understand,' Niall said tenderly. 'But know, Jess, that this is the beginning of a long, long courtship. I intend to lay siege to your heart—for however long it takes. Until death do us part, if it comes to that.'

She met his eyes. They locked onto hers and the tenderness she saw behind his gaze made her heart swell.

This man. . .

Her heart. . .

Her home. . .

'My little joey needs his bed,' she whispered tremulously. 'Please, Niall. . . Will you take him to his bed?'

'I'll do that.' His eyes still asked a question.

Jess took a deep breath and made her lips move. 'And then. . .' she whispered. It was right. There could be no doubts in her heart when he looked at her like this. Her home.

'And then, Niall, will you take me to mine?'

'Jess. . .'

She was lifted in his arms, cradled against him, and Niall's lips met hers in a long, slow kiss of exultation.

'You won't regret this, my love,' he murmured as he carried her back over the lawn to the big French windows—and the wide bed waiting just beyond. 'I give you my word. I give you my heart that you won't regret this. From this night on. . .'

Jess woke to happiness.

Euphoria was all around her, drifting as a cloud of warmth and light and laughter. She woke with a smile on her lips and as Niall's strong arms tightened in loving possessiveness the smile grew.

'Where do you think you're going?' Niall's voice growled as she stirred and she twisted within his arms so that she could see those wicked eyes. They devoured her naked body with transparent hunger.

And she wanted to be devoured. And to devour in turn. . .

'My babies. . .' she whispered.

'You fed those pesky orphans at four o'clock and again at six,' Niall murmured into her hair. 'According to my watch it is just after seven. Therefore. . . Therefore, my Jess. . .you are my own private property for fifty more precious minutes. Agreed?'

She ran her finger lightly down his face, feeling the sheer strength of him. Glorying in the fact that he needed a shave—and he would every morning. From this day forth. This was how he would feel. . . All the wonderful maleness of him.

'What will you do with me if I say yes?' she asked him wickedly.

'Do you have any suggestions?' Niall nibbled one
ear, her nose, her lips—and then his mouth moved
downward with an intent that made her gasp.

'N-no. . .'

'Then we'll just have to think of something,' he
murmured, sinking lower and lower and Jess opened
her mouth to reply.

And couldn't.

She was all his.

He was her man.

The day intruded all too soon.

The phone rang just on eight.

It was Niall's mobile phone, tucked beneath the
pillow.

Tucked beneath two heads.

Geraldine.

Jess heard the nurse's voice come down the line and
imagined how the nurse's eyebrows would rise if she
knew where Niall was lying as he talked to her.

Heaven forbid the introduction of video phones.

Jess lay cradled in Niall's arms as he talked. She
could hear both sides of the conversation with
ridiculous ease.

'Dr Mountmarche, I'm sorry to bother you but
Ethel's started vomiting,' Geraldine was saying. 'I was
wondering whether I could give maxolon with the next
pethidine injection.'

'I'll be right with you,' Niall told her. 'I'd like to
examine her before the next injection.'

'Oh. . .' There was a short silence. 'Are you out at
the farm?'

'No.'

'But I knocked on your flat door,' Geraldine said.
'There wasn't an answer. I thought. . . Well, Sarah's
due to take over and I wanted to give Ethel the injection
before going off duty. If it's going to take you fifteen
minutes to get here. . .'

'I'm closer than you think,' Niall told her and leaned

over to kiss Jessie lightly on the nose. 'Almost. . .' He kissed again, this time aiming for Jessie's lips '. . .almost under your nose. Two minutes, Geraldine.'

'So what's she going to make of that?'

Jess lay and watched Niall dress, torn between anxiety and laughter.

'If I know our Geraldine she'll have two and two added up before I reach the ward,' Niall smiled. He buttoned his shirt, then stood and looked down at Jessie's nakedness. She didn't cover herself. She should, she guessed——but not while Niall was looking at her like that. He was glorying in her body and she wanted nothing more. 'Do you mind, my lovely Jess. . .?'

'I. . .I guess. . .'

'You'd better not,' he warned her, 'because I'm not good at being kept in a cupboard. For one thing, I'm too damned big. For another. . .' He touched her face with a finger. 'For another, every second I'm away from you is too darned long. Will you have breakfast with me, my Jess?'

'Breakfast?' Jessie's eyes widened in startled enquiry. Her body was languorously sated. She felt like staying exactly where she was——for a very long time.

'Today's Saturday,' Niall smiled. 'No clinic. And I need to go home to Paige. Feed your orphans, arrange to have them cared for for the rest of the day and come to the vineyard. OK?'

Jess smiled tremulously up at him.

'O-OK.'

'My Jess.' He paused. 'You'd best stop looking at me like that because. . .'

'Because?'

'Because you have the power to distract me like no other. Come to the farm fast, my love. I'll be waiting.'

'There's a few things I have to do.' Jessie's voice sounded strange——not her own. It was as if she'd changed in the night. 'I. . .I have to see to Ethel's dog. Maybe after breakfast. . .'

'Come when you can,' he told her. 'I'll be waiting.'

Jess fed her animals, showered and dressed in the same lazy euphoria. She couldn't make her body move fast for the life of her.

Niall was waiting.

Even that incentive wasn't enough to shift the haze of blissful languor.

She needed time to adjust. To savour. To convince herself that this was right. She'd committed herself body and soul and this time. . .this time Jessica Harvey was being no fool. She was entrusting herself to a man who was absolutely to be trusted. Who accepted his responsibilities with all due care. . .

Someone she could give her heart to and know it would be cherished. . .

She needed to see Ethel. Sarah was in the corridor when Jess emerged. She smiled at Jess and Jess knew by her smile that Geraldine had been talking.

By tonight the whole darned island would be talking.

'Is Ethel fit to see me?' she asked a trifle breathlessly.

'She's fit to see you, I reckon,' Sarah told her, her smile broadening at Jessie's obvious discomfiture. 'No policemen, though. I'm under strict orders to say she's sedated if Sergeant Russell wants to interview her.'

'Is she sedated?'

'Yes,' Sarah admitted. 'But she's awake—just— and I know she's worrying about her animals. It must only do her good to see you.'

'Is. . .is Dr Mountmarche still with her?'

Sarah almost chuckled and Jess grimaced. The start of things to come. . .

'He is,' Sarah managed blandly. 'Not for long, though. He was held up to begin with. There was a kiddy with a pea up his nose for the doctor to see as soon as he started work. . .' She cast another covert grin at Jess.

'And now Chris Hayes has rung to say his old father

had a fall in the woodshed last night and reckoned he lost consciousness for a while. Old Mr Hayes is in his own bed now and swears he doesn't need a doctor but Chris asked if Dr Mountmarche would go.'

So Dr Mountmarche would go. A man who faced his responsibilities. . .

'I hope Paige isn't fretting. . .'

'I can tell you that, too,' Sarah smiled. 'She rang in person and asked for her daddy. Quite the young lady she's getting. I heard the doctor explaining how long he'll be so she can't be worried.'

All bases covered. . .

OK. . .

So Niall was with Ethel now.

Jess smiled, not as broadly as Sarah but a smile for all that, and went to see Ethel.

Ethel was so ill. . .

The woman was propped up on pillows, her damaged hand swathed in white bandages and cradled on pillows in front of her. Niall was holding her good wrist, his face grim.

Ethel turned to Jess as the young vet entered and her eyes were wide with anxiety.

When she saw who it was she relaxed—but only a fraction.

'Barry's still in the lock-up,' Jess told her swiftly and watched some of the tension lift from Ethel's face. 'And will be for at least two days, if Dr Mountmarche has anything to do with it.'

'Two days or longer,' Niall growled. 'Jess, Ethel says she won't lay charges.' His eyes gave her an urgent message. You know this lady, his eyes were telling her. See if you can do some good.

Ethel's face was blank and lifeless. All the fight had been knocked out of her. 'I'm sorry,' she whispered. 'I don't. . . I don't. . . Jess, what am I going to do?'

'Leave him,' Jess said bluntly. 'You know you must. The only question is how—and where will you go? Ethel, what happened last night?'

'He hit me,' Ethel whispered. 'Well, that's not so unusual. He does it all the time—when his dinner's late or if he's had a bad day or sometimes if I look at him wrong. . . I don't know. . .

'Only last night Kiro, my Rottweiler—well, he's Barry's dog, really; Barry bought him because he fancied a savage dog but I feed him and Kiro reckons he belongs to me now— Well, last night Kiro got frightened and tried to bite Barry. Not really. I mean he just snarled and snapped when Barry hit me. But Barry said the dog had to be killed.

'He said. . . He said I had to do it and if the dog wasn't dead when he got back from the pub he'd kill the dog and break my other arm—and kill my horse as well. He said we weren't keeping any more animals.

'So. . .so I didn't know what to do. Kiro. . . Well, I couldn't bear it. I just locked the house and. . . Only then Barry came home and got the chainsaw and I didn't realise how drunk he was. . . I heard the noise and went over to the wall and told him not to be a fool and the next thing the saw just came through. . .'

Her eyes fell to her hand and she closed her eyes.

'I wish it had killed me,' she whispered.

Niall Mountmarche's face was as grim as death. He opened his mouth to say something—and then closed it again in a tight, fierce line.

'Sergeant Russell will want to lay charges against Barry,' Jess said gently, glancing up at Niall. 'Will you do it, Ethel?'

'How can I? He'll kill me.'

'Not if you're off the island,' Jess said staunchly. 'Ethel, where does your daughter live?'

'In Sydney. Near my sister.' Ethel's face softened. 'I've a little granddaughter now but I've never seen her. Barry won't. . .' Her voice faded to nothing.

'You need to go to Sydney anyway to have your hand rebuilt.' Niall somehow had his face under control again. 'Could you stay with your daughter or your sister when you come home from hospital?'

Ethel's eyes stayed closed. She was so close to exhaustion. This needed to be sorted though or she'd get no peace. There had to be some light at the end of her troubled path.

'There's no room,' Ethel said bleakly. 'Christine's in a flat with her husband and the baby and my sister has four of her own kids. There's Mum's house. . .but Barry would just come. . .'

'Mum's house?'

'My mother died six months ago,' Ethel said drearily. 'She always hated Barry—so she left the house to me. It's just a simple two-bedroom weatherboard but it's close to Christine and my sister. I tried to persuade Barry to move—I'd so like to be close to them—but then. . . He said I had to sell the house. I know what he'd do with the money. It's on the market but it hasn't sold. . .'

Jessie's face cleared. 'Well, then. . .'

'It doesn't solve anything,' Ethel said drearily. 'Barry would just come. He'd make it awful. . .'

'Not after what he's done.' Niall's grim voice was laced with iron determination. 'Ethel, if you're prepared to lay charges against him, we can organise an intervention order. Barry won't be allowed anywhere near you. If the house is in your name. . .'

'It is.'

'Then there's no problem. . .'

'But. . .' Ethel's eyes opened. She looked dazed. This woman had been bullied for so many years that she lacked the capacity to see any hope at all. 'My animals. . .'

'Kiro could go with you,' Jess told her staunchly. 'I'll look after him until you're out of hospital in Sydney and then we'll fly him over to join you. No problem.' Her face clouded. 'I'm not sure about your horse.'

'She'll have to be put down,' Ethel said sadly. 'I can't keep her in Sydney.' She looked up at Jess, a trace of strength returning to her eyes. 'She's in awful condition. Barry wouldn't let me feed her. Only the knackers will want her now. It's been cruel of me to keep her for so long, anyway. I kept hoping. . . I kept hoping Barry would change his mind. Will you. . .will you organise it for me, Jess?'

'I'll do that.'

'And you. . . You'll look after Kiro?'

'Absolutely.'

'And I don't have to see Barry?'

'We'll put a police guard on the door if necessary,' Niall said strongly. He loaded his syringe with a vial of pethidine. 'OK, now, Ethel. Enough organisation. We'll fix you an airlift to Sydney but meanwhile I'll give you something to let you sleep.'

'I'd like that,' Ethel whispered. 'I'd like to sleep. . . I feel like I could sleep for a very long time. . .'

'Bastard. . .'

Niall had barely got out of the room before the word erupted. His hands clenched into fists. 'Hell, Jess, how can she have put up with it for so long?'

'Victim syndrome,' Jess said sadly. 'She's so used to being abused and bullied she sees it almost as normal. To organise herself away from Barry without help would be beyond her.' She sighed. 'I'll ring her daughter in Sydney and explain what's happened. Hopefully she'll be safe. . .'

'Give me names and I'll ring,' Niall said roughly. 'I'm her treating doctor.'

'I'm treating vet.'

'So you are—bless you,' Niall smiled. He took her shoulders and gave her a swift kiss. 'But I'll do the phoning. You seem to have enough on your hands. You now have a Rottweiler among your orphans, Dr Harvey. And a derelict horse. You take on the world, my lovely Jess. . .'

'I don't. . .' To have a man look at her like that. . . To have this man. . .

'Just leave room for me in that big heart of yours,' he told her and his smile deepened. Finally he shook his head. 'Damn. I have to go. See you at the vineyard later—barring emergencies?'

'I'll be there.'

CHAPTER TEN

FIRST Ethel's dog and horse must be attended to.

The Simmonses' house looked deserted. The only evidence of last night's drama was a piece of plywood nailed over the hole in the weatherboards. Someone had taken away the chainsaw.

The house was derelict. No money had been spent on it for years.

Barry would come here when he came out of prison—and hopefully live here alone for the rest of his life. As long as Ethel could stay strong and keep him away. . .

And as long as he didn't find some other unfortunate woman. . .

A dog was whining at the back of the house. Jess walked through the back gate and the whining became frenzied barking.

'Hey, Kiro. . .'

She'd brought pacifiers if she needed them—but she shouldn't. This dog knew her; he wasn't terrified as he'd been the night before, staunchly protective of his mistress, and he was hungry.

Jess had also brought a piece of steak from the hospital kitchen.

The dog growled as she came near but as Jess didn't hesitate his growl became uncertain.

'Hey, boy. . . I've come with breakfast. And greetings from your mistress. . .'

Jess walked steadily forward, the steak in her hand. As soon as she was within reach she laid the steak on the ground and then knelt beside it.

She didn't stir as the dog ate, careful not to give him the least sign that she was a threat.

Finally the dog finished the steak and looked sideways at this intruder on his territory. Jess didn't move.

Nonplussed, the big dog whined—and then put his nose in her hand and sniffed.

'There's no more here, boy,' Jess smiled, rubbing him gently behind his ears. 'But I'll be back later with more.'

She sat for a good ten minutes, chatting conversationally to the big Rottweiler and slowly gaining his trust. As long as Barry Simmons remained in prison there was no hurry to move him. Kiro could stay on his chain here until she'd arranged alternative accommodation. By the time she took him in her car she wanted his complete trust.

He was lovely. Rottweilers had a vicious reputation but an animal who was treated well was a real pleasure. Kiro was all pleasure. His steak devoured, he was wriggling his delight in Jessie's company.

This dog could be an absolute comfort to Ethel and protection as well in case of Barry turning up in Sydney.

'I have to go,' Jess said regretfully. 'See you later, boy.'

She left him whining his own regrets and went to find the horse.

Ethel had been right when she'd said that the horse would have to go to the knackers. Jess saw the little mare and her heart sank.

What sort of penury had reduced Ethel to treating the horse like this? The only excuse for it was that Ethel looked half-starved as well. If she hadn't, Jess would have felt rage.

Even so. . . The horse should have been sold long ago rather than fall into this condition. She was in a stable at the other end of the yard to Kiro and whatever trouble had befallen Ethel had meant that the horse hadn't been tended for days.

The manger was empty and the water supply was reduced to a little fouled water at the bottom of a rusty trough.

Ethel had loved this mare, Jess thought sadly. The

woman had been so bashed about that she'd simply given up—though it was her husband's threat to her animals that had driven her to final rebellion.

'So, what do we do with you?'

The little mare looked at Jess with apathetic, dulled eyes. She hadn't been exercised for weeks, Jess guessed, and her coat was rough and unbrushed.

Jess filled the water trough and searched vainly for feed. She'd have to buy some and come back.

Or maybe it would be kinder to ring the knackery this morning.

On the mainland a quiet little mare like this might stand a chance of being sold and rehabilitated. Not here. . .

There were plenty of healthy horses on the island. No one would want one in this condition.

Jess ran her hand along the mare's bony flank. 'Be sensible,' she told herself.

It was going to be hard enough to arrange accommodation for the dog. Jess could hardly keep a horse at the hospital.

'So. . .'

'So I ring the knackers,' she told herself harshly. 'Now, before you burst into tears.'

She walked out of the stables and closed the doors behind her.

'Doc Harvey. . .'

Jess blinked as she came from darkness into sunlight. It took her a moment to realise who was calling her.

A curlered head was poking over the back fence.

Monica Sefton.

Island gossip.

'Dreadful goings-on last night, weren't they?' the woman beamed. 'I was the one that called the police. Well, I said to my Herbert, I know he bashes her something awful and you can't call the police all the time but the screaming last night—you wouldn't credit it. And then the chainsaw! How is she, poor soul?'

'She'll be OK,' Jess said briefly. She wasn't about

to fuel gossip by giving Monica any more information than she must.

'Lost two fingers, I hear. Dreadful! And what's going to happen to her animals?'

'I'll look after Kiro,' Jess told her and then hesitated. She badly didn't want to go into the Simmons's house. 'Mrs Sefton, could I use your telephone? Ethel's mare is in dreadful condition and I'll have to call the knackers.'

'Come right in,' the woman beamed. She jumped from the fence and walked toward the front gate, only her curlers visible now behind the wooden palings. She kept right on talking.

'What a shame. Such a pretty little mare she was when Ethel bought her. I remember the fuss. Ethel's mum sent her some money for her birthday and Ethel spent it on the horse before Barry knew about it. I thought he'd kill her. I reckoned he might but he only found out when the Benns arrived to deliver it. The Benn kids all came too and Barry wanted to hit Ethel so bad you could taste it.

'He and Ray had words—Ray's a big man, isn't he?—and Barry finally shut up and went down to the pub. Then a couple of Benn kids stayed on till dark to see it settled by which time Barry was drunk and the fuss just died down. Only I hear Ray told Barry if anything ever happen to the foal he'd fix him up proper. And Barry's a born coward.'

Jessica had stopped dead behind her section of fence.

'Monica, you mean the mare was originally Ray Benn's foal?'

'Sure.' Monica's head poked up again over the fence. 'It's a foal of that mare of theirs. . . You know the one—nice brown little thing the kids ride in gym-khanas. Though didn't I hear it bucked one of the kids off last weekend?'

'You did.' Jess licked dry lips. 'Mrs Sefton, I might just ring Ray Benn first before I ring the knackers.'

*   *   *

Half an hour later, Jess bade farewell to Ethel's mare.

The little horse left the same way as she'd arrived four years ago—in the Benns' horse float, surrounded by excited little Benns.

'Of course we want her,' Ray Benn practically shouted down the phone when Jess rang him. 'Jess, you send her to the knackers over my dead body.'

'She's in rotten condition, Ray.'

'Yeah, well, I never should have sold her to Ethel,' Ray said savagely. 'Ethel pleaded—and I knew she'd love her—but Barry Simmons. . .' He broke off. 'Well, least said about that slimy creep the better. We'll hook on the horse float and be right there. She's not Matilda but she's the next best thing.'

He was true to his word.

Jess stood and watched as the float was driven out of the yard. The little mare's eyes seemed lighter already.

One happy ending.

Ethel would love this. It was right.

Niall would enjoy hearing it, too.

Jess said farewell to Ethel's Rottweiler again, climbed into the car and turned the vehicle towards the Mountmarche vineyard.

Towards Niall. . .

Her heart was so full that it felt like bursting into song all on its own.

Niall's house call to old Mr Hayes must have taken more time than Jess had spent at the Simmons's. The ambulance he'd been driving wasn't in front of the house when Jess arrived.

Jess pulled into the yard and Paige came stumbling out almost at a run on her crutches. The child was still in her nightdress, her face liberally smeared with something brown.

When she saw who it was her face fell—but only for a moment.

'My daddy's not home yet,' she said importantly. 'But he said on the phone he'd be here soon. He didn't say he was bringing you.'

'Maybe because I'm bringing myself,' Jess smiled, swinging the little girl up to give her a hug. This little one could be her daughter. . .

Whoa, Jess. . .

Things were moving too fast.

Hugo appeared at the kitchen door and smiled a welcome. 'Doc should be here any time, Miss,' he beamed. 'Would you be interested in a cup of tea——or a glass of wine?'

'Neither, thanks,' Jess said nervously. 'I think——if you don't mind——I might just take a walk down to the river while I wait.'

'Good idea.' Hugo beamed. 'I think I'll come with you. I left a pair of secateurs on the bottom vines last night and I need them this morning.' He turned to Paige. 'And you, miss. . . What about hopping inside and getting yourself dressed? If your dad comes home and finds you still in your nightdress at eleven in the morning he'll think your Uncle Hugo is a very poor sort of child minder.'

Paige giggled. 'I don't think you're very good at it, anyway,' she chuckled. She looked impishly up at Jess. 'Uncle Hugo let me have chocolate ice cream for breakfast.'

'Yes, well, you can get rid of the evidence of that, too, while you're about it,' Hugo grinned. 'You'll have us both in leg irons.'

Paige didn't seem too worried. She giggled again, adjusted her crutches and hobbled inside.

'Is it OK to leave her?' Jess asked doubtfully and Hugo nodded.

'Her dressing's her one absolute independence,' Hugo told her. 'When she was still so ill and Niall tried to help her she screamed like she was being beaten. Now. . .now it takes her half an hour or more but she does it herself. And every time we let her be the happier she gets. It's like an expression of trust.'

'I guess I can understand that.' Jess thought of the changes the little girl had suffered in her life and thought that if Paige managed to retain only one measure of independence she was performing miracles.

'She's changed so much over the last couple of weeks,' Hugo smiled. He was leading her down the rough tracks between the vines. 'An easier little girl all round. I reckon we've turned the corner.' He looked at Jess out of the corner of his eye. 'Thanks to you, I reckon.' He grinned. 'It's starting to look like our Dr Mountmarche might put down a few permanent roots.'

'You don't think he intended to. . .before. . .?'

Before what? What was she trying to say here? Before Jess?

The elderly man hadn't heard her question. He stared out over the vineyards, his face reflecting satisfaction.

'He'll come back now,' he said placidly. 'Before. . . Well, Niall just came to see Paige right—and to make sure the girl's claim to the vineyard couldn't be refuted.'

'"The girl's claim". . .?'

'This vineyard belongs to Paige,' Hugo told her. 'You knew that, didn't you?'

'No.' Jess stared. 'I thought it belonged to N. . . Dr Mountmarche. . .'

'Heck, no. Not that he—well, we—didn't want it.' Hugo shook his head. 'Louis Mountmarche was an old bastard. He screwed as much money out of the family as he could to set up this place and did his brother— Niall's father—and me out of a lot in the process. Ran up debts in our names and then skipped the country.

'Well, that's water under the bridge—thirty-year-old history. Next thing we knew he'd set up here and then the place gets an international reputation. Louis knew the business better than any of us. He was the last Mountmarche in wine. With his actions he'd forced the rest of us out of the business.'

'So. . .'

'So we forgot about him.' Hugo grimaced. 'I started importing wine into Britain but I've always hankered after a place like this. Niall's father left the business completely. And then Louis died. . .'

'Leaving the winery to Niall. . .'

'No. To Paige. . .'

To Paige. . . Jess frowned. 'I. . .I beg your pardon?'

Hugo shrugged. 'Louis hated our family with a vengeance. Well, there was a lot of bad blood. Niall's father tried to sue for money owing and Louis acted like he was being personally persecuted. Niall's father went broke in the process. Anyway, Louis decided he hated Niall's dad and he hated me but Niall was old enough for Louis to remember.

'Leaving the vineyard to Niall would be like leaving it to Niall's father but I guess at the end he couldn't bear to leave it away from his blood. So he wrote a will leaving it to Niall's children—if there were any children—or otherwise it was to be sold and the money given to the Seamen's Mission. Not that Louis ever had anything to do with the Seamen's Mission. It was just pure vindictiveness on his part.'

Jess stopped still and stared.

'So because Niall had Paige the vineyard came back to the family?'

'Well, that's the good part.' Hugo smiled. 'We— none of the family—knew Paige existed. Not even Niall. The papers were being processed to transfer the vineyard to charity when that monk or whatever he was phoned. We couldn't believe it. The vineyard just coming back to us. . .'

'So. . .'

There was a rotten taste starting at the back of Jessie's mouth and her head felt thick and dull. She couldn't make herself ask anything else.

Hugo didn't need prompting.

'So Niall got over to Nepal to the hospital where Paige was being kept and brought her home. Took all sorts of fuss before he could prove she was really his daughter. The lawyers put him through hoops. . .'

Jess swallowed and swallowed again. 'So. . .so he proved she was his daughter so he'd get the vineyard?'

'Well, of course,' Hugo said solidly. 'Anyone would. This place. . .' He gazed about him. 'You don't know it, miss, but this place is a gold-mine. This part of the island seems to have soil and a microclimate made for growing grapes—better, I reckon, than the Bordeaux region of France. And it's ours again.'

'Paige's.'

He didn't hear the strain in her voice. Hugo touched a budding branch with a gnarled hand and grinned again.

'The Mountmarche family's,' he corrected himself. 'I'll build this place up so even Louis wouldn't recognise it. By the time Paige comes of age. . . Well, with luck, it'll be doing so well we'll have bought more land and turned all the northern slopes into vineyards.'

'And. . .and Niall. . .?'

Hugo shrugged. 'He'll be off back to England, I guess,' he told her. 'He's a damned fine doctor, miss. Got a great reputation as a surgeon already and he lectures at the university and writes books as well. In time, when the child's settled and Niall has to go, maybe we'll find a nanny.' He smiled slyly across at her.

'But the way our Niall's been looking at you— Well, if he had a wife on the island to look after Paige then we wouldn't need a nanny—and he might even come back and forth from time to time. He'd have to if you were here. And you and me could cope with Paige and the vineyard. . .'

'You and me. . .' Jess whispered. 'While Niall goes back to London!'

Hugo paused. He'd almost been talking to himself, Jess realised. Now he turned and saw her face—and his own face dropped.

'Look, miss. . .' he said uneasily. 'That's just what I've been thinking. I mean. . . Paige thinks you're wonderful and you're well settled here—part of the island. . .'

'And I'd make a good mother for Paige. . .'

'She loves you already,' Hugo said simply.

'I don't believe this.'

'I shouldn't have said anything.' Hugo shuffled anxiously. 'Heck, miss. . . It's none of my business. I mean, I don't know what's between you and the doc. I was just thinking—when he didn't come home last night—'

'That he might have been finding a nanny for Paige.'

Hugo had taken a tentative step forward again but Jess didn't move. She stood with sunlight glinting on her face and her world crashing around her feet in a million razor-sharp pieces. Her nails were clenched so hard into her palms that she found later they'd drawn blood. 'Hugo. . . Hugo, I'm not coming further. I. . . I've changed my mind about waiting for Dr Mountmarche. Tell Paige. . . Tell Paige I'm sorry. . .'

And she turned and ran up through the rows of budding vines.

Hugo stood watching her with horror.

'Miss, please. . .' His elderly voice cracked with despair as he yelled after her. 'Miss. . . Jess. . .'

It was no use. Jess was beyond hearing.

Jess absented herself for the rest of the day.

She'd arranged for her animals to be fed until six so she took the radio in case of emergencies and drove herself down to the beach.

She sat on the sand and watched the surf run in and out while she tried to force her wounded mind to think.

It was like she'd been beaten.

Two men. . .

She'd given her heart to two men and one had turned out to be a murderer and the other. . .

He'd used a little girl to get a vineyard.

What lies had he told her?

Had he known of Paige's existence before? Who knew? It was likely that he had, Jess thought bitterly, but had only acknowledged it when his precious winery was at stake. The Mountmarche wine.

So he'd brought his puppet owner back to Barega

along with Hugo to do the work—and then he planned to head back to England. The family would be wealthier and he could get back to his precious career.

And Jess?

Jess tried hard to make herself think logically.

Why would he want her? Why not a nanny?

She licked dry lips, the answer being so darned obvious that it hurt.

Paige was a wealthy little girl. If Karen reclaimed her. . .

Karen had deserted her child when Paige needed her most. Any judge would look favourably on Niall's custody claim—especially if he'd provided her with a stable stepmother.

If Jess took over that role then it would leave Niall free to do what he liked.

Men!

Jess stood up and walked down to the water. She stood in the shallow breakers, kicking sand and foam up in a vicious spray before her.

'I should have known,' she whispered. 'I'm no better than Ethel. The victim syndrome. . . No man I want is any good. No man. . .'

So where did that leave her?

Right back where she'd started. Alone.

Only this was worse than being alone. What she'd felt for John Talbot—the fledgling feelings of admiration and love—were nothing to what she'd felt for Niall Mountmarche.

It was as if part of her was shrivelling inside—and she knew that it could never grow again.

The end. . .

'So, it's back to your animals,' she told the sea bleakly. 'They need you. . .'

And what about Paige?

Her heart went out to the lonely little girl living with the two men—men who saw her as a tool to get what they wanted.

Paige had to stay on the island. Her family's plans dictated that.

'I can be close to Paige when Niall's not on the island,' Jess whispered to herself.

And for the next few months? The time Niall had promised to be medical superintendent for the island? They had to keep some sort of professional relationship.

Heaven knew how.

Jessie's heart was like stone. She glanced at her watch and was stunned to see how late it was.

She had to organise Kiro before six. . .

'OK, Jess,' she said bleakly as if someone was listening. 'Get on with the rest of your life. A life without Niall Mountmarche. . .'

Why did it seem like no life at all?

Kiro at least was delighted to see her.

The dog wriggled his pleasure. Jess fed him and took him for a swift run at the nearby beach before tying him up for the night.

In the morning she'd take him to the hospital and kennel him in the unused chook run. If she took him to a strange place tonight he might howl the hospital down while he became accustomed to new surroundings.

She radioed Sergeant Russell briefly to assure herself that Barry would be locked up until then.

'He'll be in for at least another couple of days,' the policeman said with satisfaction. 'Ethel lodged a formal charge before she left for Sydney and there's not a lot of folk round here ready to provide Barry with bail.'

'Ethel's gone. . .?'

'Doc Mountmarche arranged an air ambulance transfer this afternoon. I helped take her down to the airstrip.' He hesitated. 'You know who else did?'

'Who?'

'Ray Benn and a couple of the Benn kids. They came to see her to tell her how happy they were with the horse. Dunno who howled the most. Ethel or Ray.'

Jess heard the smile in the big policeman's voice and a tiny light lit up inside her. There were still glimmers of happiness left to her.

Embers instead of flames.

'What am I going to do, Kiro?' she whispered but the big dog had no answers.

He reckoned he had problems of his own.

'Yours will be over soon,' Jess told him, giving the dog a fierce hug. 'Someone still loves you. We'll send you to Sydney to be with your mistress as soon as we possibly can.'

If only someone could magic Jessie away as well. . .

There was no one. Of course there was no one. No one for ever. . .

She left Kiro looking mournfully after her and drove back to the hospital.

The hospital held little appeal as a destination. At a guess, the place would be empty. If Ethel had gone and no more patients had been admitted then the hospital side would simply close down until needed. The staff could take three deep breaths and a holiday.

Niall Mountmarche wasn't on holiday.

The island's medical superintendent was waiting for her, sitting on a fallen log behind the hospital car park. Heaven knew how long he'd been there. He had the air of a man in no hurry at all.

As she pulled to a halt he rose and walked slowly towards her.

Niall stopped at the car-park barrier.

'Jess. . .' His voice was a caress.

Jess closed her car door with a bang and locked it with careful deliberation. 'I don't want to see you,' she said, her back turned to him.

'Why not?'

'If you don't know, you should.' She took a deep breath and turned, bag in hand, to walk down the path into the building. Niall blocked her path.

'Jess, Hugo told me. . .'

'Told you what?' Jess stopped dead, cold anger welling through. She felt so betrayed that it made her feel sick. 'That I was upset? Did he tell you that he told me the truth? And I didn't like it?'

'Jess, let me explain.'

'There's nothing to explain. Let me past.'

He gripped her shoulders and stopped her pushing by. She was no match for his strength. One hard shove told her that. Finally she stopped pushing—instead, standing still and rigid—steeling herself not to respond to him.

'I think there is.'

'No.' She fought back stupid, betraying tears of weakness. 'Dr Mountmarche, does or does not the vineyard belong to Paige?'

'Yes, it does. But. . .'

'The whole island believes it's yours. And you let them believe that.'

'It was easier that way,' Niall told her. 'Jess, it'll create problems for Paige. . . If her mother finds out. . .'

'You mean it'll create problems for you,' Jess spat. 'Maybe even a custody battle. Was I to be the insurance?'

His face stilled. 'I don't know what you mean.'

'It'll be easier to keep Paige—keep the vineyard—if you have a nice docile little wife living on the island,' Jess whispered. 'Wouldn't it?'

His face darkened with incredulity. 'I didn't think that.' His grip tightened so much it hurt. 'Not for a moment. Jess. . .'

'You want to go back to England?'

'I don't know,' he told her. 'My medicine's important to me and with two doctors already on the island I can't see any permanent place for me here. I can write but I don't want to lose my medicine completely. But Paige is important, Jess. Once she's settled and happy, if I have to go then she'll come with me. And I hope. . . Jess, I hope you, too. . . I won't leave you.'

'Pull the other leg,' Jess said crudely. 'It plays

''Jingle Bells''. Let me past, Niall Mountmarche. I want nothing to do with you or your corrupt little schemes.'

'You have to believe me, Jess.'

'I don't,' Jess said bluntly.

She met his look and anger met anger.

The incredulous expression in Niall's eyes was slowly hardening to a cold, hard contempt.

'There has to be trust, Jess.'

'Well, there isn't. I've seen what men can do and I don't want any part of it.'

'You can't compare me with that. . .with. . .'

'I do,' Jess spat. 'John Talbot. Barry Simmons. Niall Mountmarche. Underneath, they're a type. Well, I'm damned if I'll spend the rest of my life with men like that. You. . .you talked Ethel Simmons out of being a victim. I have only myself to get me out of this mess. And I will. Now get out of my way, Niall Mountmarche, before I scream blue murder. Now!'

The hostility in her own eyes was reflected in his. There was tight-lipped fury.

'If you think I'm capable of that, there's no more to be said,' he said harshly. He released her so fast that she almost staggered.

There was a long moment of silence. Jess met his look unflinchingly.

Then, finally. . .finally, Niall Mountmarche stood to one side of the path, giving her room to pass.

'We had it all, Jess. . .'

Jess shook her head as she made her feet walk past him.

'We had nothing.'

CHAPTER ELEVEN

IT WAS a night of loneliness.

A night of pain.

A night so long that Jess never wanted to go through it again in her life.

Jess somehow managed to get through her normal tasks. She drove out to the Benns' to help settle the little mare in her new home, hoping that it might help ease the hollow ache inside—but nothing would.

Nothing.

She lay in the dark in the empty hospital and she'd never felt so alone in her life.

When the telephone rang at three a.m. it was almost a relief.

She'd rather have a difficult calving in the middle of a paddock than this awful emptiness.

It wasn't a sick cow.

It was Sergeant Russell, sounding anxious.

'Jess, are you safely locked up there?'

Jess frowned. She leaned over and switched on her bed light.

'What. . .? How do you mean?'

'Barry Simmons is out.'

'Barry. . .' Jess frowned. 'You mean he got bail?'

'I don't mean anything of the sort,' the sergeant said wearily. 'There was a car crash over the other side of the island. Drunk teenagers. No damage to themselves but a lot of property damage. I had to go. Barry must have heard me go and used the opportunity to fool Marie.'

Marie. . . The sergeant's wife.

'What happened?'

'He started screaming blue murder five minutes after I left. Said his hand was killing him—said the bandages

168

the doc put on his hand were cutting off circulation and his fingers were turning black. When Marie went down to the cells he made out he was having some sort of convulsion—grabbed his hand, choked and fell over like he was unconscious. So. . .' He sighed. 'So she broke every rule in the book and went in. And he hit her and took off.'

'Is she all right?' Jess asked anxiously.

'Sore, sorry for herself and feeling stupid,' the policeman told her. 'But he locked her in the cell and she was there for an hour till I got home. So, now. . . Well, I guess he'll probably head home. I'll go there now.'

Jessie's heart missed a beat. She should have taken the Rottweiler out of harm's way. 'Sergeant, Kiro. . . Ethel's dog's there. Barry threatened to kill it.'

'Yeah. He's angry enough to do anything,' the sergeant said. 'The only worry is, he's furious at Ethel. He knows she's laid charges and I didn't tell him she's left the island for Sydney.'

'You didn't tell him. . .?'

'I haven't been able to get within earshot of him for abuse since he found out Ethel was laying charges,' the sergeant said. 'I couldn't have told him even if I'd wanted to. Which I didn't,' he said fairly. 'After treating Ethel the way he has the least he knows about her whereabouts the better. But now. . .' He sighed.

'Jess, if he thinks she's still at the hospital. . .he could come. Just make sure the place is locked. I'll check the house and be right with you. Ten minutes. But lock the place, Jess.'

'It already is locked.'

'You're sure?'

'Y-yes.'

'That's something, then. But Jess, be careful.'

He hung up, a worried man.

So what was Jess supposed to do now?

Go calmly to bed?

Jess had been wide awake before. Now she was so

alert that every noise was magnified a thousand times.

The place was locked. Only staff had keys.

It was a rambling building. If Barry broke a window on the far side——on the hospital side. . .

The policeman would be here within ten minutes and Barry Simmons would surely only break a window to gain access to the women's ward. If he found his wife gone. . .

Jessie's ears strained. There was something banging over in the other wing. A gentle thumping that was so soft that it had been in the background and she hadn't heard it.

An intermittent thumping. Like a French window banging gently in the wind.

It shouldn't be open. The nurses were under strict instructions to leave the place locked.

But Niall had been back this afternoon.

Niall, whom a woman would be mad to trust. . .

She would go mad by herself here with a window open so close. Jessie bit her lip in indecision.

This was stupid. Barry Simmons was no threat to her. Even if he broke in he didn't want Jess. He was angry with his wife. There was no need to think that the man was intent on violence to anyone other than Ethel.

'So lock the window,' Jess told herself harshly. 'Before you go nuts.'

She opened the door out into the corridor and stepped out into the darkened hospital.

It was definitely one of the French windows banging.

Out here she could hear it clearly. It was a wonder that she hadn't heard it earlier in the night——but maybe the wind had only just risen.

She walked slowly down the corridor, nervous despite herself. The light switches were near the nurses' station. Jess flicked them and the place lit up.

The light should have reassured her. Instead, it did no such thing.

It increased her sense of urgency.

There was a smell. . .

Petrol.

The hospital reeked of petrol.

Dear heaven. . .

Jess flung open the door into the women's ward. This was where the sound had come from. The French windows were open wide and, as she watched, the breeze caught them and swung them gently closed with the thump she had heard.

If the place smelled of petrol. . .

The smell was unmistakable. She should get out. Jess walked quickly over to the windows and out onto the verandah.

There was nothing here.

So why the smell?

She frowned. She had to be right. The smell couldn't be from a small container. It was stronger in different places—and there were dark, damp patches on the floor.

Even out here on the verandah there were damp splotches—and the lock on the French windows was splintered and broken.

Barry must have been here. . .

Maybe he still was. If he'd poured petrol around the place. . . There was only one reason why he'd do that. To set fire to the building. . .

There was no fire yet. Maybe he'd put the petrol down and changed his mind. Discovered that his wife wasn't here.

But if a spark ignited the petrol. . .the place would go up like a bomb.

Jessie's heart froze in fear.

Her animals—Wilfred and tiny Wobble—were still inside.

Things—buildings and contents—could be replaced but not her wallaby and wombat. Jessie looked frantically back into the hospital, her mind racing.

From out here it looked safe—normal—but there was no ignoring that smell. She wasn't going back through the corridors. If the petrol caught she'd be trapped.

She'd go around. Break a window from the outside and get back into her flat that way. Even if she was imagining the smell. . .

A light cut through the night, lighting the verandah where she stood. Jessie turned to face it. A car was screeching to a halt in the car park and a dark figure emerged.

It wasn't the police sergeant. Jess could pick this profile anywhere.

Niall Mountmarche. . .

Niall could obviously see Jess on the verandah and Jess could discern relief in the way his shoulders sagged.

Sergeant Russell must have phoned him. . .

Why, for heaven's sake? What use was Niall Mountmarche, except to upset her still further? Jess didn't want Niall. She wanted only to concentrate on her animals.

What help was he?

Jess turned again toward the broken French doors. Not that way, she told herself fiercely, blocking out Niall's presence. Don't be stupid, Jess. . . You'll have to go around the verandah. . .

She took one step forward toward the verandah steps—and the world exploded around her in a brilliant, molten rush of engulfing flames.

She woke to damp earth and dazzling light.

Someone was pushing her face into the grass. Jess had a mouthful of the stuff and it was threatening to choke her.

There was a weight on top of her, bearing her down.

Blind panic took over.

Frantically Jess fought against the weight and, instead of being pushed down, the weight rolled aside and she was being pulled into strong, fierce arms.

'Lie still, you little termagant. Dear God, Jess. . .'

'Let me go. . . Let me go. . .'

She could see Niall's face above her now, glowing in reflected flame. There was soot on his jaw and his forehead—black grime, deeply embedded—and Niall's eyes were dark slits.

'Jess, you're burned. Hurt. Lie still.'

'I'm not burned. . .' Jessie's face was tingling. She put a hand to her forehead and felt singed hair. 'I'm not. . .'

'The explosion knocked you out on the verandah. I got you off just before the roof came down.' Niall's arms held her close and she could feel a shudder run the length of his body. 'Dear God, if I hadn't been here. . .'

'B-Barry. . .' Jessie's voice was a choked whisper. 'It must have been Barry. . .'

'He's torched the place.' Niall was using his body to shield her from the worst heat. Now he shaded his face with one hand to try to see. They were lying full length on the lawn and the heat was sweeping over them in waves. 'God knows where he is. Jess, there's no one else inside, is there? Think.'

'No. . . No one. . .'

Yes, there was. . .

'Wilfred. . .'

Frantically Jess tried to haul herself away from Niall's encircling arms to see. The fire was all through the front of the hospital—but Jessie's flat was at the rear. Maybe. . .

'Let me go,' she screamed. 'Niall, let me go.'

'Wilfred?' Niall's voice was blank. He was still lying prone, his arms restraining her with absurd ease.

'My animals. They're in my flat. Let me go!'

'If you think I'm letting you go near that. . .'

She lashed out then, shoving with fists and elbows and feet, clawing like a wild creature. The attack was fierce and unexpected and Niall's hands released their grip for a fraction of a second.

It was all she needed. Jess was on her feet and

running barefoot, her charred nightgown tattered around her. If she could get through the garden. . .

Jess was lithe and fit and running was something she could do well. It would take Niall Mountmarche a mammoth effort to catch her, especially as she knew her way round every inch of this garden.

She had to beat him. She couldn't let him stop her.

The heat was almost overpowering. The wind was coming from the north, pushing her along with its blast and Jess knew that most of its strength was from the fire.

There was no saving the hospital now.

There were only her animals.

She couldn't let them be incinerated. They trusted her absolutely. She was all they had.

They were all she had. . .

Heaven knew what Niall was doing. She couldn't care. Jessie's feet flew, careless of flying cinders or gravel on the paths. Here was the gate to the back yard—and here the path leading to her flat door. There was a glass pane in the door. If she smashed it. . .

The flames weren't here yet. Soon. . .

The smoke must be unbearable inside. . .

Jess stooped to grab a rock by the path and raised her arm to smash but her arm was stopped in mid-air.

The stone was lifted effortlessly from her nerveless grasp.

'What the hell do you think you're doing?'

Niall's voice was hoarse with smoke. She could hardly see him for billowing clouds of acrid fumes.

'I'm going in.'

'The hell you are!'

'They'll die,' Jess sobbed.

'Jess, they're animals.'

'Yes, they are,' she screamed at him. 'And they're helpless. They're locked in their pouches. They depend on me and I can't let them die. . .'

'You can't go in. OK, it's not burning yet but if he's spread the petrol. . . Jess, it could go up any second.'

'I'm going in. There can't be petrol. I was in there while he was spreading it.' Frantically she fought him, wild with grief.

Fighting was useless. The only reason she'd broken from him before was because she'd surprised him. This time he was ready.

Niall stood holding her against him in an iron grip, one of his hands holding both of hers behind her back and the other encircling her body.

'You don't care,' she sobbed. 'You don't care about anything.'

'I care about you. And you'll die in there.'

'So what?' she screamed. 'At least I'll die trying— and they need me. No one else does. It doesn't matter about me. Let me go!'

'Jess, you haven't even got shoes on.'

'I don't care. Let me go.'

He took a deep breath then and steadied. His dark eyes perused her frantic face. 'Tell me exactly where they are, Jess. The same place as I saw them last night?'

'Why?'

'I'm going in.'

Jess stared through frantic tears. 'You. . .you can't.'

'I can. Tell me, Jess. The same place. . .?'

'Y-yes. But. . .'

'Stand back, then.' Niall stooped to find Jessie's rock again, then raised his arm with it held high.

The world was turning somersaults. He couldn't. He didn't care. . .

'No!' She clutched his arm and he paused for a fraction of a second. 'Niall, you'll be killed.' Jessie's voice broke in fright. It was OK for her. But for Niall. . .'No!'

'Better me than you.'

'But. . .'

'Don't you understand?' Niall said fiercely. He smashed the rock into the window, sending a shower of glass into the room. 'It's me or you. And if you die. . . It'd be a damned sight better to be dead myself.'

'But Paige. . .'

'She has Hugo—and you. Look after her like you look after your wild animals if anything happens to me, Jess,' he said roughly as he hauled himself up and over the sill. 'That's all I ask. Don't follow me in. Promise me, Jess. Promise!'

'I. . .' Jess could hardly make her voice work for confusion. She felt dizzy and sick with fear.

He paused for a fraction of a moment.

'Promise.' It was a harsh command.

'I. . .I promise,' she made herself whisper.

'My love. . .'

Niall leaned to give Jess one last fierce kiss—a kiss that bruised her lips—and then he was gone.

What followed was the worst three minutes of Jessie's life. She stood by the shattered window, fighting for breath through the smoke, and her world shifted crazily on its axis. Shifted and spun so fast that she was in danger of falling off.

This wasn't the Niall Mountmarche she'd condemned.

This man. . .

This man was risking his life for her animals. For two wild creatures.

She heard him coughing desperately as he stumbled through the room and smoke was pouring from the shattered window. It was all Jess could do not to climb in after him.

Crazy. . .

She had to force herself to stay outside.

She couldn't go in because of Paige.

One of them had to be safe for Paige. Niall had made her promise and she had.

Please. . .

Please. . .

There was the sound of shouting from the other side of the building, frantic through the roar of flames. She opened her mouth to scream a response but no words came out.

How could it?

There were two hands at the window, a closed pouch in each.

Jess seized both pouches and laid them gently on the ground.

Then she took Niall Mountmarche's grimed and bloodied hands in hers and helped him out of the window.

Somehow they got away from the fire.

They lifted the pouches back onto the lawn and staggered back away from the worst of the smoke.

There were no words said. When the wriggling pouches were laid on the lawn, safe, they turned as one to watch the end of the Barega hospital.

The flames were in possession of the building. Their smashed window was spewing smoke with fiercer and fiercer force—and then crimson flames spurted through the gap and the shattered window disappeared into the fireball that was once the hospital.

Jess could no longer bear to look.

She turned her face into Niall's chest and wept.

The whole island was in the hospital grounds by the time the building subsided to a massive pile of glowing embers. The local firefighters were joined by every able-bodied man and woman on the island, and a few kids and dogs as well.

Jess and Niall were surrounded by a group of horrified well-wishers.

Well-wishers or not, there was nothing that could be done to save the hospital.

Geraldine's daughter appeared out of the night and took Jessie's charges back to her mother's house.

'They'll be better off away from this,' Lucy said fiercely, 'and I've formula there I took home when I looked after them last time.'

Jess could only be grateful. She had nowhere to take them. She had no home.

She stood in the protective circle of Niall's arms and she couldn't stop shaking.

'T-tell me if they seem stressed,' she managed and Lucy looked at her dubiously.

'I know who seems stressed,' the teenager said. She peered into the pouches. 'I doubt if these two even knew there was a fire. It'd take a bit for smoke to get through all this wool. Good grief, though, Dr Harvey. You should see your face.'

'It's burned,' Niall agreed. He held Jess close. 'I'll get you away from this.'

'I don't know where to go. . .'

'You'll come home with me,' Geraldine said out of the darkness but Niall shook his head.

'No. I'll look after her. . .'

'Begging your pardon, Dr Mountmarche. . .' Geraldine directed a torch down to Niall's hands '. . .but you need looking after yourself. How did you cut your hands?'

The broken glass on the window. . . Jess stared down at the bloody lacerations on Niall's strong hands and a convulsive tremor shook her.

'They're nothing,' he said harshly.

Someone had brought a blanket and Niall was holding it round Jess, keeping her vaguely decent in her tattered nightdress and holding the night chill at bay. Her feet, though, were still bare on the damp lawn.

Niall swore.

'Enough of this.' Regardless of his damaged hands, Niall lifted Jess strongly into his arms. 'I'm taking the lady home.'

'But. . .' Geraldine was made of stern enough stuff to defy even Niall Mountmarche '. . .who'll look after your hands, Dr Mountmarche?'

Niall smiled then, an exhausted smile with the strain showing through but a smile for all that.

'I've just the lady in my arms to look after me,' he said softly and his weary eyes were a caress. There was no fight left in Jessica Harvey and Niall knew it. 'Will you look after me, my Jess?'

'I. . .'

'After I've finished taking care of you, that is,' Niall added, and kissed her tenderly on her singed hair. 'And that, my love, is going to take a very long time. I think maybe a lifetime. . .'

The rest of the night passed in a blur.

Jess sat in the front seat of Niall's Range Rover and tried to make herself think.

There was no way that her mind would work.

Niall drove with one eye on her and the other on the road. As she shook he swore softly into the night.

'You shouldn't have been in that damned place alone. Never again. . .' He was talking more to himself than to her but his words sank home and were somehow comforting.

In the terror of the night somehow things had changed.

The tilting world had somehow righted itself again.

What she'd learned of Niall that morning—dear heaven, was it only that morning?—had seemed crazy. Out of balance.

And in one mad night the balance had been righted.

She huddled tight within her blanket, trying to keep her teeth from chattering, but deep inside a warmth was settling and spreading with a speed that put a petrol fire to shame.

Niall Mountmarche had risked his life for two little animals.

For her. . .

This was no man set on finding a convenient mother for his daughter. There were easier ways than trial by fire.

She ventured a glance sideways up at him and found his eyes on her—and the warmth grew.

Her chattering teeth stilled.

'Niall. . . I'm sorry. . .'

Niall lifted his hand and laid it tenderly on hers.

'Don't be. We'll have you warm in bed soon, my love,' he said gently and the warmth engulfed her totally.

After that. . .

Hugo was waiting, frantic with anxiety. Sergeant Russell had contacted Niall and asked him to go to the hospital—just in case—and ten minutes later Hugo had seen flames shoot skyward.

He couldn't leave Paige and Niall's mobile phone wasn't working. On investigation Niall found that it was missing—torn off some time. . . Consumed by flames.

Hugo's face when Niall finally brought Jess out of the car said a thousand words.

Niall carried Jess into the big master bedroom and laid her on the bed as if she was made of fragile china. Then he and Hugo cleaned and washed her burns. Her eyes were carefully checked and her throat and her burns coated with antiseptic cream.

'I'm giving you something to stop the pain and make you sleep,' Niall told her as Jess drifted in a haze of unreality.

'I don't need anything. . .'

'Remind me to ask next time I want a vet's advice on what my patient needs,' Niall said softly.

He gave her an injection she didn't feel, pulled soft blankets up to her scorched face and then sat by her side until she drifted into sleep.

CHAPTER TWELVE

HER love was still beside her when she woke.

Jess blinked and blinked again as consciousness flooded back. The sun was streaming through the north-facing windows. Niall was bathed and changed and there were dressings on his hands.

Niall can't have sat there all night.

He must have gone.

But he'd come back.

That was all that mattered. He'd come back to her.

Jess opened her eyes wide and stretched a hand out to her love.

He didn't take it.

Instead, Niall gathered all of her to him, lifting her tenderly to cradle her against him.

'I was beginning to think you'd sleep till tomorrow.'

She smiled, her face cradled against the soft cotton of his shirt. Life was immeasurably good.

'What time is it?' Her voice sounded like a frog was down her throat and Niall smiled.

'That's a very sexy husk,' he told her. 'Smoke inhalation. It'll fade, more's the pity. It's very fetching. It's twelve noon, my love.'

'Twelve. . .'

Jess pushed herself away from Niall and stared. 'You're kidding.'

'Would I kid about anything so important?'

'I. . .I have no idea.'

'Well, it's time you did.' Niall's smile slipped. He sat back and his eyes held hers. 'Jess, you are my own true love,' he said softly. 'My lady in a million. My chance of happiness. If you don't think you can trust me then I don't think I can bear it. Yesterday. . .'

'Don't. . .'

'It has to be said,' he told her. 'There were some rotten accusations floating round yesterday. One is that I used my daughter to gain this vineyard. Not true. I never wanted this vineyard. I found out about Paige and I brought her home at the same time my family were discovering the terms of my uncle's will. They put it to me that the vineyard belonged to Paige and I had no right to keep her from her inheritance.

'I was trying to find some place where Paige and I could get to know each other and this seemed the right place. That's all, Jess. . .'

She believed him. She knew now. Her heart was to be trusted and she trusted this man with all her heart. . .

'Niall. . .'

'I never wanted to come here,' Niall continued. 'But now I'm here. . . And last night. . .' He shook his head. 'This is your place, Jess. I can't see you caring for your native animals in central London—unless you take pity on a few pigeons or stray cats. And Paige, too. . . I'm seeing how much this place can give her. She's grown in health and, since she's met you, she's grown in happiness. . . So. . . If you could bear to marry a medical writer instead of a medical practitioner then maybe I'll force myself to change direction. . .'

Marry. . .

Jess lay back on her pillows and her eyes filled with tears.

'I'll go to London with you, Niall,' she whispered. 'I'll go anywhere. . .'

'We'll talk about this later,' he said gently, 'but there are things in my life more important than medicine.'

'Niall. . .'

'Hush.'

She shook her head. There was something really important she had to say. 'Niall, Quinn and Fern—the island's regular doctors—have asked if you'll consider practising here,' she whispered. 'In partnership. Fern's pregnant and there's a huge tourist complex starting. You. . .you wouldn't be very busy. . .'

He stared. 'When did they make that offer?'

'A week or so ago.'

He eyed her suspiciously.

'So why are you telling me now?'

Jess flushed. It must be the drugs Niall had given her, she thought. She was away on cloud nine.

'Because. . .because. . .'

'Say it, my Jess. . .'

'Because I'm sure I want you to stay,' she whispered. 'If you will. . . Or if you go—take me.'

She was gathered again into the safe haven of his arms.

'If I will,' he whispered softly into her mass of charred curls. 'How can you ask anything so absurd. . .?'

Jess slept away most of that day—and the next. It was as if her body was recuperating from more than just the shock and the burns, though they were enough to dictate rest.

The following afternoon she finally asked Niall for a mirror—and was appalled.

The explosion of petrol had taken the skin from her forehead and singed all the front of her hair. Her nightgown must have caught fire but luckily she'd fallen forward and the force of her body against the verandah had smothered it.

Her face was puffed and swollen. She looked like she'd been crying for a month.

'How can you love me when I look like this?' she whispered.

'It's not what you look like but what you feel like that's stopping me from loving you,' Niall grinned. 'If I thought a quick squeeze would result in anything more than a yelp of agony I'd be back in my bed like a shot. . .'

'Is this. . .is this your bed, then?'

'Our bed,' he smiled lovingly. 'As soon as I can get a ring on your finger.'

'Oh, Niall. . .'

'You've been incredibly lucky.' Niall was carefully applying cream to the few areas of blistered skin.

'Do they know. . .? Have the police found Barry?'

'We assume so.'

Jess stared. 'What. . .what do you mean?'

'Barry must have underestimated the power of petrol,' Niall said grimly. 'We think he broke into the hospital at the French doors and went through the place splashing petrol. Maybe he thought Ethel was there and we were hiding her. Who knows? Maybe he just thought up a plan and then couldn't think of a better one when she wasn't there.

'We assume he smashed open the laundry door to make an exit and then threw a match on the floor. The petrol did the rest. We found what we think is his body trapped in the ruins of the laundry.'

'You think. . .?'

'It's burned beyond recognition. I went down this morning to make a dental report,' Niall grimaced. 'The dentist flies in from the mainland twice a month so the report has to be sent to Sydney for matching against records. But there's little doubt.'

'I. . .I see.'

'Are you up to facing visitors?' he asked her.

'Niall. . . Looking like this?'

'You look beautiful,' he told her.

'Says you.'

'And who are you to argue with your affianced?' He kissed her carefully on her unburnt chin. 'Back to the case at hand. Visitors or no visitors?'

'Who. . .?'

'The whole world is clamouring to see you,' Niall smiled. 'I think every islander and their dog, cow, pig, hen or whatever has sent their best wishes, by phone or in person. Your cousin and his wife—Quinn and Fern, is it?—have rung on the hour every hour demanding I care for you as if you were more precious than diamonds. And I'm to tell you Fern is flying over in person tomorrow to make sure her orders are carried out.

'I'm also to inform you that there's no problem with insurance and the hospital rebuilding started yesterday. Every islander worth his salt is beavering at the site as we speak. Also, Lucy has brought first-hand reports of Wilfred and Wobble's glowing good health. And. . .'

He hesitated.

'And?'

'And my small daughter is aching to see you. I didn't let her in until now—because I thought she might want to touch you.'

'Because. . .' Jess sat up in bed, winced at the sudden movement and positively glared at her love. 'There is nothing I want more than to have Paige touch me.'

'You're sure?'

'I'm sure.'

He smiled and walked across to open the door.

'Paige. . .'

Paige had been waiting. She stood on the threshold, her eyes enormous.

'Wow. . .' she whispered. 'Jess, you look awful.'

'The swelling will go down soon,' her father promised her. 'It's really our Jess in there.'

'You. . .you like my new hairstyle?' Jess whispered.

The little girl swung herself across on her crutches to touch the frizz that had once been Jessie's fringe. Her fingers were feather light.

'Oh, Jess, does it hurt?'

'Only when I laugh,' Jess smiled.

'Then you mustn't laugh.' Paige's face was dead serious. 'Hugo and me have made you some soup for tea. Do you think you'll be able to eat it?'

'I'm sure.' Jess leaned forward and kissed Paige lightly on the face and Paige pulled back.

'You mustn't. Your lips look all sore. . .'

'Not too sore to kiss.'

'No. . .' She looked like she doubted it. 'Jess, Daddy says you'll probably stay with us for a while.'

Jess looked shyly up at Paige's father and her cracked lips smiled. 'If that's OK with you, sweetheart.'

'Yep.' She grinned, her equilibrium recovering nicely. 'All sorts of people come to our farm now. They come to our home,' she corrected herself. 'Daddy's taken down the sign—and we even leave the gate open. We have to. Geraldine came about three times. She put four stitches in Daddy's hand and I watched. And she came this morning to make me exercise my legs. And you know what she said?'

'What did she say?'

'She said seeing we've a new invalid in the house it's time I learned not to be one.' She gave a nervous giggle. 'So. . .'

'So?' Jess looked a question up at Niall but he was clearly as bemused as she was.

'So, look what I can do.' Paige crowed. She carefully laid her crutches on the floor and turned to her father. 'Be ready to catch me,' she warned. 'I'm not too good yet.'

And she took four shaky crutchless steps forward before falling into her father's arms.

'Paige. . .'

Niall was hugging his daughter close, his arms proud and possessive.

His love was almost a tangible thing.

How could Jess have ever attributed base motives to this man? Jess lay back on her pillows and her eyes filled with tears.

She must have been mad.

'My Paige. . .' Niall swung the child round and kissed her soundly. 'My little woman. My Paige. And my Jess. I have two precious women in my life now.'

'Daddy. . .' There was a sudden hushed silence. Paige looked from Jess to Niall and back again and something in their faces must have shown as clear as day.

'You're not going to marry Jess, are you?' she asked tremulously. 'Daddy. . .'

'What do you think of it as an idea?' Niall asked. He set his daughter on her feet again and steadied her on her crutches, then knelt before her. 'It seems to me. . . It seems to me good things have happened to the Mountmarches since we met Jess. She's like a medical prescription. Prescription—one Jess. How about, pre-scription—one bride?'

Paige considered, her face pink with pleasure.

'Could she be my mummy then?'

'What about it, Jess?' Niall demanded and swung Paige round to face her.

'I'd love to be your mummy,' Jess whispered. 'If you'll have me.'

'I've always wanted a mummy,' Paige whispered. 'I didn't know I always wanted a Jess type of mummy but I do.' She hesitated. 'If you're a bride, can I be a bridesmaid?'

'I won't be a bride unless you're a bridesmaid,' Jess swore.

'With pink frills and a bow. . .a bow. . .a bow something.'

'A bouquet?'

'Yes.' Clearly this was a source of immense satis-faction.

'We'll prepare you the biggest, brightest and most beautiful bouquet ever been known to grace a wed-ding,' her father promised. 'Two bouquets. One for you and one for my bride.' Niall's hand came out to take Jessie's and his eyes were giving her messages that didn't need to be spoken.

'And. . .' Paige limped forward and leaned her crutches on the bed. Her small hand came out to claim Jessie's from her father.

'I mightn't be very good at getting dressed in a pink frilly dress with a bouquet,' she confessed. 'I'm not very clever at buttons and stuff. But. . .but if I had a mummy, then my mummy could help me get dressed.'

'That's a mummy's job,' Jess said seriously and her tears brimmed over and splashed down her burned cheeks. 'My job—if you'll have me.'

'Jess, you're crying.' Paige looked anxiously down at Jessie's wet cheeks and then up to her father. 'Daddy, Jessie's crying. Make her stop.'

'I know just the remedy.'

Niall knelt down and took both his women into his arms. He kissed Jess softly on the lips, mindful of her bruising but Jess would have none of it.

She put her arms around Niall's neck and deepened the kiss, savouring the tiny pricks of pain. Savouring her love.

They kissed for a very long time and when they finally drew apart, Jess was no longer crying.

'See. . .'

Niall smiled down at Jess and his voice when he spoke was not quite steady. 'See, Paige. I can fix crying.'

'By kissing?'

'By loving,' Niall said softly. 'It's the very best cure.'

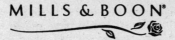

MILLS & BOON®

Medical Romance™

Books for enjoyment this month...

TRUSTING DR SCOTT	Mary Hawkins
PRESCRIPTION—ONE BRIDE	Marion Lennox
TAKING RISKS	Sharon Kendrick
PERFECT PRESCRIPTION	Carol Wood

Treats in store!

Watch next month for these absorbing stories...

THE REAL FANTASY	Caroline Anderson
A LOVING PARTNERSHIP	Jenny Bryant
FOR NOW, FOR ALWAYS	Josie Metcalfe
TAKING IT ALL	Sharon Kendrick

Available from:
W.H. Smith, John Menzies, Volume One, Forbuoys, Martins,
Woolworths, Tesco, Asda, Safeway and other paperback stockists.

Readers in South Africa - write to:
IBS, Private Bag X3010, Randburg 2125.

MILLS & BOON®

Weddings ❖ Glamour ❖ Family ❖ Heartbreak

Weddings By De Wilde

❖

Since the turn of the century, the elegant and fashionable DeWilde stores have helped brides around the world realise the fantasy of their 'special day'.

Now the store and three generations of the DeWilde family are torn apart by the separation of Grace and Jeffrey DeWilde—and family members face new challenges and loves in this fast-paced, glamourous, internationally set series.

For weddings, romance and glamour, enter the world of

Weddings By De Wilde

—a fantastic line up of 12 new stories from popular Mills & Boon authors

OCTOBER 1996

Bk. 1 SHATTERED VOWS - Jasmine Cresswell
Bk. 2 THE RELUCTANT BRIDE - Janis Flores

Available from WH Smith, John Menzies, Volume One, Forbuoys, Martins, Woolworths, Tesco, Asda, Safeway and other paperback stockists.